NAMELESS

-A Renegade Star Story-

J. N. Chaney

BOOKS BY J.N. CHANEY

The Variant Saga:

The Amber Project

Transient Echoes

Hope Everlasting

The Vernal Memory

Renegade Star Series:

Renegade Star

Renegade Atlas

Renegade Moon

Renegade Lost

Renegade Fleet

Renegade Earth

Renegade Dawn

Renegade Children

Nameless: A Renegade Star Story

Standalone Books:

Their Solitary Way

CONTENTS

One...7

Two 28

Three 37

Four...51

Five..61

Six..68

Seven...80

Eight 86

Nine...101

Ten 115

Eleven..125

Twelve..145

Thirteen 155

Fourteen 169

Fifteen 186

Sixteen..202

Seventeen 233

Eighteen 254

Nineteen...274

Twenty..300

Epilogue..309

Author Notes 313

About The Author...315

ONE

The refectory smelled like fish and old bread.

Clementine nudged me in the ribs with her elbow and nodded at the food line. "Hey, Abby," she whispered. "They got a new serving lady. Check it out."

"Really?" I asked, dropping my jaw in disbelief. I glanced up and across the room, spying a woman I'd never seen before. She dropped a scoop of brown sludge onto an eight-year-old's plate.

"I heard it's because the old one was stealing the donations and hiding it in her room," Clem said with her mouth full of food.

I glanced at a few of the nuns, who had lined up together near the far end of the dining hall. "Wow," I muttered and then secretly wondered if the food would somehow taste differently today.

My eyes flicked upward again. Sister Mable had just entered, holding a pad. It was one of the only tech pieces allowed here. The sisters liked to say that holos and pads were bad for the soul, but Sister Mable used them when she couldn't find a physical copy of a certain book. It wasn't too popular with the rest of the nuns, but I didn't think she cared.

Another thing she used the pad for was the adoption records. That was why everyone's eyes were on her at the moment.

"Good evening, children!" Mable said once she reached the head of the room.

"Good evening, Sister Mable," came the mixed response. The younger kids, sitting closer, responded enthusiastically. The older kids only mumbled. After all, we'd been through this routine a hundred or more times, and our expectations were close to zero.

Mable cleared her throat before speaking. "One of our top donors messaged me to say that they're coming to visit us tomorrow, so I want everyone on their best behavior when they arrive. They'll be here in the morning to sit in on your classes. Let's do our best to show how thankful we are for their generosity." She smiled broadly, looking over the whole group at once.

I still wasn't sure how she did that.

Mable smiled, and it seemed to set the room at ease. She was older but not gray yet. I'd tried to ask her about her life, but she always changed the subject.

I liked Mable quite a bit though, as did everyone else in this place. It was hard not to.

She began to leave, and I jumped up from my seat, moving quickly to intercept. There was still food on my plate, and I knew full well that someone else would gobble it up by the time I got back.

"Sister Mable?" I called, catching her attention.

Her covered head whipped around to see me, and she offered me that smile again. It made me feel warm and annoyed at the same time, like nothing I could do or say would affect her at all.

"Yes, Abigail?" She made a point of greeting every child by name, unlike the rest of the adults. They only remembered a few of us, like how Sister Mackavoy always used Clementine's name but only called me "child".

I flushed and looked at my feet. "These donors coming tomorrow, do you think they'll, um, want to adopt?"

Mable tilted her head, pausing for a second before coming closer to lay her hand on my shoulder. "To tell you the truth, they didn't say. But it's always a possibility. They already have a child of their own, but they may have it in their hearts to bring another member into their family. Let's be optimistic, shall we? One never knows what the future will bring."

If they were looking to adopt, it made sense that they would want a *younger* child. There was a reason why kids older than ten were almost never adopted.

I smiled but felt a sinking feeling in my chest.

Mable seemed to read my mind, and her hand squeezed my shoulder gently. "Chin up, Abigail. Keep your head held high. There is a family out there for all of you. We simply need to find it."

I scowled. "There *was* a family for me. They just didn't want me in it."

The squeeze tightened. I looked up at Mable, and she glanced down at me with firm, yet kind eyes. "Then they weren't the family for you. Stay true to yourself, my dear. The gods always bless those with kindness and honesty in their hearts."

I'd heard things like that a hundred times before. Coming from Mable, though, I somehow wanted to believe them. I put on a brave smile, fighting back the tears that had begun to form.

In a way, I *did* have a family, even if it was only the other kids in this orphanage.

Growing up here was all I remembered. I had been given away too young to know my parents. I had vague memories of a brown-haired woman, an uneven smile, and the smell of cinnamon, but I didn't know if those were real.

It was probably just a dream.

I walked back toward the table and got about halfway there when the bell rang, telling us it was time to head back to the dorms. All the children got in line. As I joined them, I felt

Clementine's hand slip into mine, giving me a lukewarm piece of bread.

"Saved you a roll," she whispered as we started moving toward the exits. "What was all that about, anyway?"

"Just needed to talk with Sister Mable about something," I said, feeling my belly rumble with sudden hunger. I fought the urge to gobble down the bread, choosing to save it for when we were back in our dorm.

"It must have been important," Clementine said, careful to keep her voice down.

"It was," I whispered back, giving my friend the same warm smile I'd seen on Sister Mable, and suddenly, I felt okay.

* * *

I turned in my bed, looking at Clementine in hers. "All I'm saying is that even if we don't get adopted, we still have the chance to get into one of those Union schools."

"What good is that?" she asked.

"It just means we don't need a family to make it," I explained.

Clementine turned in her bed, and even through the dark, I could see the annoyed look on her face. "Yeah, and you don't need a stupid flipping shuttle to get to the other side of a planet, but it sure helps."

My eyes widened. "Clementine," I whispered. "You better

be careful before one of the sisters hears you using bad words."

"And you notice how I'm just an angel when they're around?" Clementine tucked her hands under her chin and smiled adorably.

She *did* have a gift. She could fake the innocent little girl routine on demand. With her smooth skin, full lips, and straight black hair, she looked like one of the angels painted on the windows downstairs.

Unlike me. I had trouble keeping my unruly blonde hair out of my face. With my pale skin, everyone seemed to take turns asking if I was sick or not.

Sometimes, I thought it was weird that Clementine and I were friends. We'd had neighboring beds for as long as I could remember, so maybe it was just a coincidence. She was outgoing, impulsive, and energetic, and I wasn't.

"It's just, we've been waiting here all our lives, and it makes me think that nobody wants us," I whispered. I leaned back in my bed, looking up at the ceiling. I couldn't tell what this room used to be. It was tall, with massive windows that stretched across the whole wall, and long enough to provide space for two rows of single beds.

"You need to stop it," Clementine grumbled, laying her head on her hands. "It's like you've given up already. We have plenty of time." I heard the sound of fabric rubbing on fabric and turned my head to see her stepping off her bed and finding her slippers. "I'm going to get some cookies."

I propped myself up on my elbow and tilted my head. "Cookies? You have cookies?"

Clementine was already on her feet. "The lunch lady that got fired had to turn in all the food that she'd been saving. I know where they put it. You in?"

I slipped out from under my blanket and sat up, my feet dangling from the edge of the bed. "I can tell you that the sisters aren't too happy with girls who wander the halls after bedtime."

"All the sisters have turned in for the night already," said Clementine.

I leaned forward. "They have a night watch—"

"I'm going whether you're coming or not. And I'm not saving any for you."

I rolled my eyes before slipping out of bed and finding my slippers. We quietly made our way to the heavy wooden door, which was cracked open at all times. It was a quick trip down a flight of stairs to the kitchen. We scurried down the steps as quietly and as quickly as we could.

No one was out right now, so we made it to the kitchen in under five minutes. It wouldn't be long before someone came along, so we'd have to be quick and snag our cookies while the snagging was good.

The food, mostly donated non-perishables, was stacked high on the shelves. "In here," Clementine whispered, kneeling under one of the shelves deep in the back and producing a pair of plastic, sealed packets.

She tossed me one, and I opened it quickly. The smell of the baked goods had my mouth watering, and not only because I'd left my dinner unfinished. The rare smell of cocoa and walnuts made my stomach growl, and I took one of the six treats and crammed it into my mouth.

"So good," Clementine whispered, biting into the cookie.

"Almost makes you happy that they caught her, doesn't it?" I asked.

Clementine snickered, nibbling on her second one. "I could eat these all night."

"We can always come back down tomorrow night for another—" I paused, my head snapping around to face the door that we had entered the kitchen through. Clementine was looking in the same direction, which told me that she had heard it too; a door opening and closing somewhere close by.

"Get under the counter," Clementine whispered urgently, tossing her half-empty packet underneath as she spoke. "If they ask, I'll just tell them that I came to get some water. They won't like it, but it won't be a problem. It's not like they can tell us not to drink water, right?"

I shrugged and didn't argue. Clementine was a quicker thinker and a better liar than me. She was our best chance to get out of this free and clear.

I ducked under the kitchen counter, grabbing Clementine's cookies and curling up. I watched the shadows of the room as the distant footsteps grew closer. After a few short seconds, the door swung open, and I saw a figure step inside.

"Hello?" a woman's voice asked. "Clementine? What are you doing up and about at this hour?"

"Sister Mackavoy," Clementine said, and she sounded surprised. No, almost afraid. "I-I just needed a glass of water. I'll go back to bed now. Um, if that's okay."

I didn't like Mackavoy very much. Few of the girls did. I didn't like how she always seemed to find something for me to do—to keep my hands from being idle, she said.

Mostly, I didn't like how she always took Clementine away to her prayer room. She called Clementine her "special helper", but I didn't understand what that meant or why she needed one. Later, when I would ask Clementine about it, she would always change the subject.

"Nonsense, my dear," said Mackavoy. I could see from the shadows that she had stepped in closer, her hand coming up to stroke Clementine's hair. "I was just on my way to fetch you." The sister's voice had taken on a warm, strange quality.

"Oh, of-of course, Sister Mackavoy," Clementine said in a soft, suddenly feeble tone. "If we must."

"We certainly must, my dear," said the sister. "Now, come along." She wrapped her arm around Clementine's shoulder, and they started walking toward the door.

Mackavoy turned back around before they reached the hall to turn off the light. When she did, I saw her pause for a moment, shifting her weight as she leaned in my direction. "Now, who's there under the counter?"

I froze with a sick feeling in my stomach. There was no way she could see me, right? I wasn't moving or making any sounds. I wasn't—

"I can see your foot, child," Mackavoy said, letting a warning note enter her voice. "Come out." The nun stepped in closer.

The stern voice jolted me from my thoughts, and I complied quickly. I stood up, still holding both packets of cookies, my back straight as I kept my eyes low.

Mackavoy shook her head. "I'm so disappointed in you, child. Stealing from the orphanage's food stores is a very serious offense." She came closer, dragging Clementine with her, and she grabbed my chin, forcing my head up to look at her.

She seemed so angry, but there was something more to it, like a hunger in her eyes.

"Only bad girls steal from the pantry," she said. "And bad girls must be punished. Wouldn't you agree?" She glanced over her shoulder at Clementine.

"Y-yes, Sister Mackavoy," Clementine said, her eyes wide and afraid.

The woman turned back to me. "Do you agree, child?"

"Yes, Sister Mackavoy," I answered. I tried to swallow but found my throat dry. We never should have come down here.

"Good," the sister said. Her finger moved from my chin to my lips, then to my cheek. Her fingernail hurt when she pressed it against my skin, but I tried not to flinch. "Come now, the both of you. We need to see you punished for your transgressions. The gods are not pleased with you, and we must rectify this."

She turned around, putting her hand on my shoulder and pushing me in front of her. Oddly, we were heading toward Mackavoy's room, not the prayer rooms on the other side of the massive building. A cold feeling crept into my gut and spread to my arms.

I looked around as we entered through the wooden door. Clementine kept her eyes on the floor, with her hands clenched and her body tense as she walked to the nearby couch against the far wall. I'd never seen my friend look like that, and I couldn't shake the sick feeling of dread in my belly. I regretted every step I'd taken since we'd left the dormitory.

"Clementine knows what to do," said Mackavoy. "Follow her lead and take a seat." Despite the politeness of her tone, the hand on my shoulder was tight and firm, her fingers digging into me. She pushed me towards a couch, causing me to briefly stumble before I caught my footing and continued forward.

I sat beside my friend on the sofa—dark red with a purple trim—and the nun smiled, giving Clementine's hair a stroke before finally shaking her head at the both of us.

"Now, petty thievery might not seem like such an awful thing, but stealing a crumb is the same as stealing a loaf. All sin is the same in the eyes of the gods, and so you must receive the same punishment, too." She walked away from us and went to her dresser, opening the highest drawer and retrieving a wooden paddle.

My eyes snapped to Clem. "W-what's that for?" I asked, even though I already knew the answer.

Clementine said nothing.

I looked back at Mackavoy, and she turned to us, a smirk on her face. She slid her free hand along the edge of the wooden paddle like she was examining it.

"I-I'm sorry Sister Mackavoy!" I exclaimed. "We won't do it again! I promise!"

The woman held up a finger to her lips. "Now, now, child. You must be quiet, or the penance will increase."

I could feel my heart beating as my breathing intensified, but I still found the strength to shut my mouth. Maybe if I did what she said, she'd let us go. Maybe this was just a test to see if we were obedient. Maybe this was all for show.

"Clementine," said the nun. She pointed at her, twirling her finger.

Clementine stood up, a flat expression on her face, and began to unlace her gown. It gently fell to the floor, and I closed my eyes.

I felt terror jolt through me. This had to be a dream. I must still be in my bed, wrestling with a nightmare, trying to wake up.

"Abigail," Mackavoy said, raising the paddle and pointing it at me. "Your turn."

"B-but..." I was having a hard time speaking, the lump in my throat getting bigger, choking my voice. What was this feeling I had? I couldn't keep my hands from shaking.

"Don't make me tell you again," said the nun, her tone less sweet, less gentle, like all the goodness had drained from her in the last few minutes, gone to some other place.

I looked at Clem again, trying to get some kind of response, but she only stood there, staring forward, an empty expression replacing the girl I knew. I forced myself to stand, then undid my lace, taking my time with it as I tried to find a way out of this.

But what could I do? I was being punished for something I

did. It wasn't a mistake. It wasn't a lie. I'd stolen food, so it was my fault, wasn't it? If one of the other sisters saw this, they'd probably agree that I deserved it.

I tucked my arms from the sleeves and let the garment fall to my feet, and I closed my eyes again.

"Now, sit," said Mackavoy.

I swallowed but did as she said. I wanted to go away from here. Something about this felt wrong.

"You girls all think you deserve everything," the sister continued. She eyed the two of us, letting her words linger for a while. "You deserve *nothing*. Do you think I had it this easy when I was your age?"

"No, Sister Mackavoy," said Clementine. Her voice was almost monotone.

With my eyes still closed, I tried to imagine another place, another time. I did it sometimes during class when I got bored. But this wasn't dull. It had my full attention in all the worst ways. I'd have to struggle to escape it, imagining myself anywhere but inside this room with this woman.

"So very ugly," said the woman. I peeked my eyes open to see her scowling at us, slowly shaking her head. She looked disgusted like we were garbage. "Clementine, turn around and accept your punishment."

Clem got up and did as she was told, placing her hands on

the sofa as the sister raised the paddle. I closed my eyes and turned away. I heard the paddle come down hard, the sound of it so loud it filled the chamber like a thunderclap. I flinched with every blow, increasingly afraid as my friend received her blows. Through it all, Clem barely reacted. She never made so much as a grunt or a cry. No quivering sounds. She was stronger than me, braver. She was like a different person, and I didn't know why.

The whole time, I pictured myself in a place with my mother and father. They were laughing and smiling, and I was doing the same. We were happy together, so far away from this place, maybe on another planet in another star system. I could almost smell my mother's perfume, a blend of roses and jasmine. It was exotic. A perfect fit for a woman so beautiful.

"Abigail," a voice said, piercing my daydream and forcing me to stir. "It's your turn now."

I cracked my eyes open, slowly looking at Clementine at my side. She had turned around and sat quietly in her spot, saying nothing.

Mackavoy raised the paddle. "On your feet, girl."

"I, um, p-please don't, um—" I could barely get the words out, as though the fear had scrambled my brain and twisted my tongue. The anticipation of the pain was overwhelming me. I wasn't sure I could handle this.

"Now!" snapped Mackavoy, causing me to jerk away. Her

tone was so hateful, so loud.

"B-but, I—" I pulled back, sinking into the sofa.

"Enough!" She grabbed my wrist and dragged me from the seat, spinning me around with more force than I could resist. She was so big compared to me, and so much stronger. I couldn't do anything to stop this if I wanted to. I was just a kid.

"B-but—" The tears came at last, overwhelming my senses. A warm flush ran across my cheeks as the reality of what was about to happen finally settled. This was going to hurt, and there was nothing I could do about it.

I closed my eyes, still crying, and the tears flooded out of me faster than they had in a long time. Think about mother and father, I told myself, trying to find the images again. A dark-haired woman, beautiful curls and green eyes. A burly man with a booming, jovial voice. Chocolate and walnut cookies in the oven. Those were always my favorite. They'd know that, and the house would smell of them. Mother would help me with my studies and tell me wonderful stories. I always liked books about other places. My parents would say they believed in me. We'd have a pet dog too, and...my mother would be pregnant with my baby brother.

I heard something squishy behind me, along with a few grunts, and then some kind of movement. A warm liquid sprayed against my backside, causing me to cringe and turn around.

The nun was gripping her neck, blood seeping through her

fingers. She had holes in her garments, right along the sides, and red stains were forming.

Clementine held a small knife in her hand as she stood before me, a quiet, empty look on her face.

Mackavoy's eyes began to roll back, and she stumbled forward. Clementine dug the knife into the old woman again, at least four or five times in rapid succession, each in the belly. I could hardly process any of this, it happened so quickly.

The nun staggered, almost stumbling forward. Her head bobbed, and her arms dangled like she was half-asleep. I couldn't tell what she was trying to do. She seemed to move her lips, but only mumbles came out, and even then, they were mostly whispers.

She stumbled to her left, reaching for what looked like a piece of cloth on the nearby lampstand, but missed it completely, knocking the whole thing down. The bulb shattered in a hard crash, and I flinched. She fell on her hands and knees, still trying to get to the cloth, but her hand dropped like it was limp, and she scraped it across the glass.

Her body was covered in blood, red replacing her porcelain skin. I wanted to scream, but all I could do was watch, totally frozen.

She began to crawl, this time to her desk area. Her mouth continued to open and close, although she was saying nothing.

There were only smacking, wet sounds.

Finally, when she neared the desk, she reached out with a shaking, weak arm to grab a white box, hidden in the open compartment below. She thumbed at the edge, slipping each time, and leaving a swipe of blood. The box fell over, and I saw a medical sign on the front.

Mackavoy's arms finally gave out completely, and she collapsed on her belly, tears in her eyes as they darted around the room, not focusing on anything in particular.

Clementine only stood there, a vacant expression on her face. She looked down at the nun as she struggled to breathe.

Clementine watched it all.

My eyes drifted down from my friend's face to the knife in her hand. It was the same one from the counter, the tiny blade sitting next to the fruit and the Book of Ages. When had she decided to take it? Why hadn't Mackavoy noticed? She'd had her eyes on us the entire time.

I tried so hard to yell or speak, but my mouth wouldn't even open. I wanted to ask what was happening. I wanted to ask Clementine why she had done this bad thing.

Because it was bad, right? Mackavoy was on the floor, so it had to be, didn't it?

Clementine was quiet and still, blood covering the entire dagger in her hand. She was like a different person, nothing in her eyes. No sign of the girl I knew. No emotion to tell me how to feel or what to think. Nothing but a void.

I heard the door open, but I still couldn't react. I turned my head around to see Sister Mable standing under the arch. She looked completely horrified. "Oh, my gods!"

Clementine dropped the knife. "I-I didn't mean to," she whispered, hoarsely. She backed away from the body, reaching for her clothes, which were now covered in the nun's blood. "I just wanted it to stop. I—"

Mable's eyes darted between Mackavoy and the two of us. After only a few seconds, the shock faded as she assessed what happened. She walked across the room, stepping over the body and pulling Clementine and me away. When we were near the door, she returned to the bed on the other side of the room, taking the sheets and wrapping us both. Before I could ask what was going on, she'd placed us inside one of the hallway closets. "Stay right here. I'll be right back. Do you understand? Nod if you do, girls. Please, you have to listen. Do you understand?"

We both nodded.

"Good," she said, quickly, and looked around. "Stay here."

Clementine's lip began to tremble, and her eyes welled up with tears. "I didn't mean it."

Mabel nodded. "I know you didn't, Clem. Please, just stay here."

She closed the door behind her, leaving us in the dark. We didn't say anything, but my eyes drifted down to my hands. They were clean. Clementine's were still red and wet, but mine were still so clean.

I didn't have the cookies, I suddenly realized. I'd left them back in the room.

"I need to go back," I said in a hoarse whisper. "I left the cookies on the couch."

"What?" Clementine asked. There wasn't much light, but I could still see the confusion in her eyes.

"We can't leave the cookies back there," I said, my voice a bit clearer. "I need to get rid of them. We'll get in trouble if anyone finds out we—"

Clementine shook her head firmly. "No, Sister Mable told us to wait here. Forget the cookies, Abby."

"But—"

Mable opened the door again before Clem could answer. She was carrying some traveling bags and two sets of clothes. "Get dressed, girls. We're going on a trip. Don't worry. Just do as I say, and everything will be fine."

She closed the door again, leaving the clothes in our hands. I stripped down and dressed in the comfortable day clothes that Mable provided. "Open the door when you're ready, girls," Mable told us.

I had a difficult time getting dressed. Maybe it was the darkness of the closet, or maybe it was something else. I felt clumsy like I barely had the strength to lift my arms.

A moment later, we were standing in the hall. I felt Mable's hand on my shoulder, guiding me toward the building's door. A street lamp caught my eye. I could feel how cold it was outside, but it didn't really matter. My head was in a fog, and I didn't care enough to ask what was going on or where we were going.

I looked out the window but couldn't see much. We were in a shuttle now, moving quickly. The cold had gone away, and Sister Mable was talking quickly and worriedly through a communicator. I knew I should try to pay attention, but I was so tired, so drained, as though I'd been standing in the sun all day.

A short while later, I felt Clementine wrap her arm around me.

It was nice, and I relaxed a little more.

Two

I kept shivering from the cold, but a mug of hot chocolate helped settle that once we reached our destination. Having something warm and sweet to sip on was also relaxing, which seemed like a good thing considering the back alley building we'd managed to find ourselves at. A man had been waiting for us at the gate, opening it immediately as we arrived. It was a compound of some sort, though the darkness made the details hard to see. I had no idea where we were or the path we'd taken to get here. I didn't even know what time it was.

Mable ushered us into a room. My mind was foggy, but the chocolate helped, even if it was only a little. I sat down beside Clem on a set of stools, waiting while Mabel remained standing. After a few minutes, my eyes grew heavy, and I wanted to sleep.

The door snapped open with a hiss, causing me to jump in my seat, and I quickly focused on not spilling any of the drink. A man who wasn't very tall or good looking, but carried himself comfortably and smoothly, entered all by himself. He looked dirty, not like the priests or the clergymen. I'd never seen a man like that before.

He smiled when he saw Sister Mable.

"Mable, it's good to see you again," he said in a deep and gravelly voice, making it difficult for me to hear him, so I moved a little bit closer.

"It's been too long, Mulberry," Mable said with a smile, although it wasn't her patient smile. A happy smile, yes, but different. More familiar maybe.

Clementine shifted beside me, watching the interaction between the two just as closely.

"Have you decided to give up a life of piety and return here, where you belong?" he asked in his low voice.

Mable shook her head. "I'm sorry. You know I've never felt at peace here."

His smile disappeared. "And you know that while I *respect* your decision, I'll always hope that you change your mind. I've even tried praying a couple of times, just to see if someone was listening."

Mable giggled. "I just need your help with these two. I found them in... well, a situation." She leaned in closer and whispered in Mulberry's ear.

His eyes slowly widened, drifting to look at us. As Mable pulled away, the man chuckled. "They did *that*?" he asked, surprised. "That must have been quite a sight."

I flinched and didn't know why.

"I'm not so sure I can take them in, but maybe we can figure something out," Mulberry said.

Mable didn't seem convinced. "Just look at them. They need a place to stay, and I have nowhere else to turn. The Church will bury this and the two of them along with it. They'll be sent away to some awful place. You've heard about the government orphanages, haven't you? Delinquents, all of them."

"What sort of folk do you think we are, Mable?" he asked with a chuckle. "There ain't no one but delinquents in this place."

She paused. "Better the devil you know. Isn't that right?"

He smirked. "Is that what they say?"

"Besides, you don't have to expose them to those things. I can get you lesson materials for their education. I only need you to house and feed them. It's only for a few years until they reach seventeen."

"A few years? They're still babies," he said.

"We're twelve," said Clementine.

The old man looked at her with surprise, like he hadn't expected her to respond. "Still," he said, turning back to Mable. "Five years is a long time to babysit."

I looked away as Mulberry turned toward us again, and as close as I was to Clementine, I could feel her do the same.

"Please," said Mable, and this time her voice was soft and gentle, more than I'd ever heard from her before. She leaned closer to him, and he seemed to relax. Finally, he smiled. "Anything for you, Mable."

Mable blushed. "Thank you." She leaned in and kissed his cheek.

He smiled again, bigger and brighter than before. Mable backed up and gave him some space, allowing him to turn his attention to us.

He wasn't an ugly man, but the way all the emotion seemed to instantly melt from his face made him a little terrifying.

Clementine and I pushed back into our seats as he came to a halt right in front of us.

"Girls, I understand that you've had a busy evening," he said. "I hope to make it at least a little easier. I just need to look at you for a moment, and then we can find some beds for you to spend the night in." His voice was that same low rumble, vibrating from his chest. It seemed out of place for such a lean-built man, at least to my mind.

Clementine and I stood from our seats awkwardly in front of him.

His eyes were brown and lingered on every part of our bodies. It felt like an inspection, as if we were animals in a pet store window.

He squatted down to Clementine, running his eyes up and down her. He suddenly pressed his hands against her clothes to show what the slack had been hiding. She gasped and took a step away from him, and he moved back quickly. He didn't apologize, but I could sense he meant no ill toward her. "Not much meat on you," he remarked. "What are they feeding you at that church, eh? Scraps and slop?"

"Funding has been a problem, but they're given as much as they want," said Mable.

He scoffed. "Hardly. The girl looks like she can barely lift a knife, let alone—" He stopped abruptly, swallowing as he shifted his weight to face me. "Well, never mind. Your turn, kiddo."

He did the same to me. His touch was deft and delicate, like a doctor's, and with similar precision. I made a point not to pull away like Clementine had, but I wasn't comfortable either.

Finally, he stopped and stood to his full height—shorter than Mable, but not by much. "I can't make any promises," he said, and it took me a moment to realize that he was talking to us, not to Mable. "But I think you'll both do fine here. The work will be hard, so you'll need to build some muscle on you, but a few months of feeding should do the trick. Mabel here says she'll pass along some school supplies, so you don't turn out total fools." He cleared his throat. "That cushy lifestyle you had as orphans will be behind you. You'll have three meals a day, a roof over your heads, beds to sleep in, and warm clothes to wear, but you'll work for what you get, and you'll do right by this woman, the way she did right by you tonight."

He paused like he was giving us a chance to speak, but neither of us did.

"You will do as I say," he told us. "No questions. No arguments. If you don't, I'll toss out into the street. I've got no reason to keep you here, except what I owe to Mabel. But you? You're both nothing to me, which means it's on you to earn your place."

Clementine raised her hand. "What we will be doing here?"

He paused, and I wondered if he was considering whether to tell us or not. His face was all but unreadable. "Honest work," he said, after a time. "We do our business here, and you'll have no part in that, but we need a few sweepers and moppers, and I'll wager you two should do just fine."

I felt my jaw clenching as I imagined my life back at the Church. It wasn't the easiest—certainly not "cushy" as this man had called it—but it also wasn't the worst place to live. We had Sister Mable. We had decent food. Most of all, we had each other. There was a certain element of comfort to it, especially after living there for these past seven years. It was my home, and I didn't want to leave it behind.

I thought about the two options in front of me. Go and take my chances in the world or stay and trust this stranger to look after me. If Mable could keep us out of the government orphanage, maybe I still had a chance to make something decent of myself. If I couldn't go to a university, then maybe I could be a nun like her. Dress up in a habit and veil like all the others, take my vows, and never marry. Devote myself totally to the gods.

Mabel was so happy and kind. She helped so many people, and the world was better for her. Would a life of service truly be so bad?

No, I didn't suppose it would. I wanted to go to school, read and find my own way, but I'd be happy helping others. I wanted to be like her.

Clementine jutted her chin out, facing Mulberry down. "I'll do it," she said with fierce determination in her eyes. "And that'll be the best decision you've ever made, mister. I promise."

Mulberry chuckled, then looked back at Mable, who beamed an easy smile at Clem. The stout man gave my friend a nod and then turned to me, waiting for my answer.

I clenched my jaw, curling my hands into fists. I could almost hear my heart beating in my chest as I stared up at the stranger in front of me. I'd never decided like this—not in my whole life. No one had ever given me the chance to decide my own fate.

I didn't know what to do.

Clem nudged me in the ribs. "I—I'll do it," I blurted out, surprised at my own words. But as I said them, I realized they were right. I'd chosen best because Clem would be with me. I couldn't leave her now, not after everything.

Sister Mable frowned as I said the words, but I didn't know why. Hadn't she brought us here for this very reason? Why did she look so displeased?

"Okay, then," said Mulberry. He craned his neck, looking at the nearby door. "Pearl! Get your ass in here!"

The sudden change in his pitch jarred me, so I flinched. No more than five seconds passed before a woman appeared in the corridor. She was taller than Mulberry, with the same lean build and short black hair tied up in a bun. I couldn't tell her age, but she seemed close to Mable's.

Mulberry eyed her for a second. "Pearl, please show these young ladies to their bunks. They've had a long night and need sleep."

The woman glanced at the two of us. "Them?" she asked, balking. "I thought we were done recruiting preteens. They're barely old enough to feed themselves, and you want to—"

"They won't be working," he corrected. "Not like that. They're your new cleaning crew. Mops and buckets. Dishes and drains. You follow?"

"Ah," she said, stretching out the sound. "In that case, both of you come with me. I've got the perfect room for you, near the north wing."

"All the way out there?" asked Mulberry.

"Better that way, don't you think? Less congested," she explained.

"Ah," he said and then nodded.

Clementine followed, but I paused for a moment to look back at Mable. "Thank you, Sister Mable."

She hesitated but quickly gave a warm smile. For a moment, she looked like she had in the refectory earlier that day, and it made me want to do the same.

"You're going to be safe here, Abigail," she said, leaning towards me. "I promise you. Mulberry is going to see to that."

The gruff man chuckled, a stark contrast to a few seconds ago when he had looked so serious.

"Thank you, too, Mr. Mulberry," I said.

He paused at that, as though my politeness had thrown him, but then cleared his throat and nodded. "You just worry about doing a good job, you hear?" As I reached the door, following after Pearl and Clementine, the old man added, "And it's Mr. Pryar, kiddo. Mulberry Pryar."

THREE

Sunlight flooded my eyes, making it impossible to keep them closed and dragging me from a deep sleep. I groaned, trying to fight it. I still needed a few hours.

My eyes blinked open as I squinted at the daylight breaking through the window beside my bed. Its glare was harsh, but the warm light felt good against my skin. I pushed myself off the bed and settled my feet on the floor. Clementine was staring out the window, just waking up and still lying in her bed.

Pearl stood watching us next to the door. She wore a heavy brown coat over a dark green vest. My eyes immediately focused on the weapon strapped to her waist. I'd never seen a gun before. It was hard to look at anything else once I caught sight of that.

"Rise and shine, girls," she said, and her voice sounded different than it had last night. Had I been too tired to focus? My brain had been foggy for half the night, after all.

We dressed quickly in our day clothes. When we finished, we lined up in front of her, ready for instruction. She indicated with her head for us to follow, and we did, imitating her silence.

Memories of the night before felt vague like it had been a dream.

The truth was right in front of us, though. New place, new day, new life. I'd never seen a house like this before. Damp halls, dusty cabinets, and no sign of any children our age.

We reached what looked like a dining hall. Unlike the one in the orphanage, this one was old and dirty, and the smell turned knots in my stomach.

After receiving our plates, we took our seats. There were other people there, but none of them spoke to us. We sat alone with Pearl at our own table, eating in silence. I toyed with the mush in front of me that looked like porridge but smelled like meat.

"It's a meal mix," Clementine said after a moment of poking and prodding her steaming food.

"All the carbs, proteins, and nutrients a body needs for sustenance during the day," said Pearl.

Clementine leaned in, brave enough to taste it. She didn't look convinced. "It needs salt."

"Eat," commanded Pearl, flatly. "We have work to do."

I leaned in again and sniffed the food. It was still hot, and while the smell wasn't particularly appetizing, my stomach told me not to care, so I ate.

The taste was different. It felt like it should have been sweet, but it wasn't, and it took a few more tries to get used to that. Still, after six or seven spoonful's, I hardly noticed. Definitely not the best meal I had ever tasted, but I sure did feel better.

Pearl left us to eat, only returning once we'd finished our bowls. She carried two brooms in her hands. "Just because Mr. Pryar accepted you into the complex out of the kindness of his heart doesn't mean you won't have to earn your keep while you're here." She gestured around at the rest of the mess hall.

Clementine looked reluctant, so I decided to take the lead. I stood, dropping off my bowl at the washer, and grabbing the broom. It wasn't like I had never done chores before, even if I had shared those chores with the other girls in the orphanage.

Clementine followed my example and picked up the other broom, and we both began to sweep.

Pearl stood by and watched. She didn't seem happy about looking after a pair of girls, but that was only a guess. Maybe the scowl on her face was normal. I had no way of knowing.

With the floor swept, we moved on to wiping down the tables. Scrubbing the grease and dried-up bits of mush took forever, and when we finished that chore, Pearl was right there to hand us another. My fascination with the gun she carried faded as my muscles ached from all the cleaning.

Clementine complained about the work, grumbling under her breath. At one point, as Pearl walked nearby us, Clem raised her voice loud enough for Pearl to hear. Pearl's only reaction was an amused grin as she gave us a pair of mops and showed us into a new area to tidy up.

The high-ceiling room spanned a large area. The sheer size of it made me groan at the prospect of mopping the bare concrete floor.

Pearl glanced at my wide eyes. "Don't worry, little one. You won't be scrubbing the whole place. Not today anyway. Just clean up that mess over there."

She pointed at a corner of the room where a bunch of knives and swords were mounted on the wall. A bright blue square was on the floor with rust-colored stains appearing over it.

"What is this place, miss?" I asked.

"An exercise room," Pearl said, annoyed. "No more questions. Just clean."

I pressed my lips together firmly and did as she said.

As I worked, I thought about how every room we entered seemed empty. We couldn't be the only ones in the complex since everything was such a mess. Maybe Pearl was keeping us away from everyone, or maybe they were all out for the day. I had so many questions but decided it was better to stay quiet and observe instead.

Our midday meal of stir-fried vegetables with egg noodles and chicken, came and went in a flash. After working up a sweat, the food wasn't half bad.

The break was short, though, and we were back at it too soon, room after room, cleaning and scrubbing, wiping and washing.

Blisters formed on my hands, and my muscles burned, begging for rest. We had agreed to follow their instructions to the best of our abilities, and I intended to keep that promise, so I didn't complain.

By the time dinner came around, I was finding it hard to keep my eyes open, even though I was starving. Even more breakfast mush sounded good at that point.

To my relief, they didn't serve us mush, but chopped beef with steamed vegetables. I scarfed down my portion and eyed Clem's as she finished. I could have eaten two, maybe even three plates.

Pearl told us to rinse our dishes and sent us back to our room. We climbed gratefully into our beds, ready to let the day go.

But the second the lights flicked off, I found myself awake again, unable to rest. I tossed for ten minutes before Clem said my name.

"Hey, Abby?" she asked in the dark.

"Yeah?" I answered.

"Do you think we made the right choice, coming here? Staying here, I mean?"

I turned around, barely able to make out my friend's shape in the dim light. "I don't know. I think so."

Clementine turned to face the ceiling, rustling her sheets. "Yeah, me too," she said, softly, and then fidgeted under her blanket. "I'm just glad *you're* here with me. It's nice to have someone to work with, even if it's just stupid sweeping and cleaning."

"Me, too," I told her.

She turned to face me, propping her head up on her hand. "Hey, I just realized something."

"What?" I asked.

"We're sharing a room, and it's just the two of us now. It's kinda like we're sisters. *Real* sisters, you know?"

I smiled at the sound of that. "You think so?"

"Definitely," she said emphatically. "I'm technically older, so I'd be the big sister, but that doesn't matter. You both look after each other. That's what sisters do."

"I've never had a sister before," I said.

"Well, now you do!" she said like that was the end of it.

A flush ran down my chest. I felt so excited. "Okay!"

We both giggled at the idea.

Clementine straightened up. "Now, there are rules about sisters, just so you know," she said, very seriously. "For starters, it means we gotta stick together, no matter what."

"Right," I said with a firm nod, although I knew she couldn't see me.

"And being sisters—that lasts forever. It's not something you can just change your mind about."

"I never would!" I insisted, partially sitting up in my bed.

"Okay," she said, and I could almost hear her smile. "Then, as of now, we're real sisters. If anyone asks, that's how it is. You and me, Abby."

"You and me, Clem!" I exclaimed, so excited that I could barely contain it.

Clementine rolled back into her bed, and I rolled back into mine. We laughed together, there in the dark of our room, smelling like soap and talking about all the things we would do when we grew up.

And whatever they were, we decided we would most certainly do them together.

* * *

It felt like I had only just closed my eyes when the shock of bright light struck me again. I sputtered, jerking up to sit. I growled, shifting my covers to the side and pulling myself out of bed. Clementine needed a bit more convincing, but she joined me after some complaining.

"Rise and shine, princesses," Pearl said, a small smile on

her face. "We've got another long day ahead of us."

Once dressed, we marched back to the mess hall, but this time, there were other people there.

Some were dressed in the same green vests and heavy coats as Pearl. They gave us odd looks, and their conversations stopped as Clementine and I made our way to our seats, but the novelty soon wore off, and they turned their attention back to whatever they had been talking about before.

After enduring another serving of the meal mix, we followed Pearl through a handful of hallways. I rubbed my sore palms in response to memories from the day before, but the room that Pearl led us to wasn't one that I had seen before.

There were two desks with work pads on them, and there was a screen at the front, with a chair in the corner. Pearl simply moved to the chair, indicating for us to sit at the desks.

Once we did, the screen lit up and showed the poorly rendered face of a man.

"Hello, Abigail. Hello, Clementine. My name is Angus, your instruction V.I. It is my privilege to take up your education and continue it to completion. You will note that your pads are already tuned to my instructional programming for easy access."

I looked down, seeing the pad light up. Thankfully, Angus's face was absent from my personal screen. The V.I.'s dead eyes were creepy enough just staring at me from the front of the room.

"I have a record of your academic achievements thus far, as well as a brief of your current educational status, and as such, I am fully equipped to handle your education as per Mulberry Pryar's recommendations."

I looked at it and then the pad in front of me. The sisters had handled all of our education in person. I'd heard about some schools that could afford a personalized V.I. for the students. Was this one of those places? It didn't seem like a school to me. At least, it hadn't resembled any school that I'd ever heard of.

"If you would kindly look to the pads in front of you, we can begin with a light review of what your studies should have covered thus far. We'll be starting with mathematics." Angus's voice sounded vaguely human, but there was a robotic undertone.

Clementine raised her hand. Angus took a few seconds to respond. "How may I help you, Miss Clementine?"

"Can we keep the pads?" she asked.

My eyes widened. I had never had a pad of my own before.

"They are educational tools and, as such, should be kept on your person at all times. So, to answer your question...yes." The V.I. smiled and immediately resumed the teaching program. I saw Pearl rolling her eyes as she pulled her own device out.

"If you'll kindly look at the pads in front of you, we can start with a light review..."

We spent the next two and a half hours on things that we

already knew: basic mathematics, quickly followed by a review of Osiris's three official languages, as well as a history lesson, complete with a visual aid that replaced the creepy V.I.'s face for a little while.

Finally, the lesson ended. "Thank you for your attention, Miss Abigail, Miss Clementine, and I look forward to seeing you tomorrow. Goodbye."

The screen went dead.

Pearl stood up, taking a moment to stretch before turning back to us. "Thank gods that's over."

She motioned for us to follow her, and I rubbed my hands, expecting more cleaning to come. I was right.

Clementine and I had the task of scrubbing down the dining hall after lunch, and then we moved over to cleaning the dishes. The kitchen had its own regular staff, but they weren't around right now. I guessed they only did the cooking. The cleanup apparently fell to us.

By the time that Pearl escorted us to our room after dinner, I felt like I could sleep for a week. The door closed behind us, and I changed into my night clothes, placing my dirty clothes in the laundry basket. When I finally settled into bed, I pulled my new pad out of my pocket and activated it.

I pressed the button on the side, lighting up the display. Angus's face appeared, but not moving like it had in the classroom.

Instead of speaking, everything he said came up as type on the screen.

The face was still creepy, though.

I spent a few minutes fiddling with the device. I had never had one of my own, but I'd handled one before and had a basic grasp of how it worked.

After tinkering with it for a few minutes, I learned that the pad could only do the education stuff that Angus allowed. I decided to look over the list of study topics the pad had access to. They were almost identical to the ones we'd seen in class. But then I saw another category at the bottom, called Fiction and Supplementary Material. I tapped the words, and a drop-down list appeared. I scrolled through them, surprised by the number of available titles. There had to be at least a few hundred here. *The Adventures of Marco Grim, The Renegade and the Duchess, Digging Forward to Tomorrow: One Man's Journey into the Ground*. The list went on and on.

I could hardly believe it. The tiny library back in the Church had been so small. We'd only had a few books, and hardly any of them had been fiction. The only exceptions were a few fables and a book of fairy tales.

My eyes stopped on one of the titles, and my chest fluttered. *Tales of the Earth: Mankind's Lost Homeworld*.

I felt myself squeeze the sides of the pad in excitement.

This was the same book that Sister Mable had read to us—my favorite book in the whole library.

"Time for bed!" barked Pearl from outside the room.

Clementine tossed in her bed at the sound of the woman's voice.

I wanted so badly to ask if I could stay awake and read, now that I'd discovered these books, but I knew better than to upset Pearl when she was in a mood like this. I'd have to wait to get my story fix until later, maybe during class. Besides, I really was tired.

I flicked the pad off, turned onto my stomach, and closed my eyes. I lay there for a while, slowly drifting, but my mind stayed on the books inside the pad, and I found I was still too excited to sleep.

After a short while, I heard voices from outside the door. Clementine was asleep, and she let out a light snore with her leg hanging off the bed.

I couldn't help but listen intently to what was going on outside, and the longer I did, the more familiar the voices became.

"It's an iffy job," Pearl said. "Still not sure why you took it. Strange choice, Mulberry, even for you."

Mulberry? We hadn't seen him since we'd first arrived. I got out of bed and crept to the door. "It tickled me," he said. "Someone wants Michael 'The Mako' Dunn taken care of? It sounded like a joke at first, but the client was sure as shit serious about it. Guess you could say that made it even funnier."

"Well, I ain't laughing," Pearl growled. "It's going to take a lot of resources, and you know that's too high profile for us. Can't you just tell him to find someone else?"

"And ruin our reputation with the Kahns? They're an untapped gold mine, and you know it. Most of their operations are done in-house, but they're giving us a chance to capitalize on their recent...personnel problem."

"It's too risky," Pearl said, quickly.

I slipped out of bed, taking slow and quiet steps as I edged my way closer to the door.

"If you don't want the job, give it to Rose," Mulberry said. "You know how bored she's been. She'll do whatever you throw her way."

"You don't think I can handle it myself?" Pearl's voice took on a sort of edge that had me leaning closer.

"On the contrary, you can handle anything the godsdamn galaxy throws at you. That's why I gave those two kids to you."

"Don't remind me," Pearl scoffed. "You ought to know better than to stick me in a house with a couple of girls and tell me to play Mother."

"Shit, Pearl, I know that, but who else is it gonna be?"

"Someone who spent the last two decades baking pies instead of slitting throats."

Mulberry chuckled. "Maybe so, but the way the world is changing, I'd say those two needs exactly the kind of lessons that only you can give them," he told her. "And I think you know that."

Their voices drifted as they began to move again, and I went back to my bed.

Slitting throats? I thought, letting the heaviness of my tired eyes finally get the better of me. *I wonder what she meant by that.*

FOUR

Another day, another dawn wake-up call from Pearl. Another class from Angus after breakfast, and another few hours of cleaning before lunch.

The days came and went, and the blisters on my hands became callouses. My sore muscles, while still aching, seemed to be comfortable with the constant work. It wasn't exactly hard labor, but I liked to think we were earning our keep.

After lunch, instead of cleaning the mess hall, Clem and I were back in the kitchen again on dish duty. From the look of the plates, I guessed they were too dirty for a simple run through the machine. We were given heavy gloves, massive brushes, and told to make them sparkle.

I still wasn't sure how many people lived in this place. So many came and went, and only a few had grown familiar. I didn't know who any of them were, and when I asked, Pearl only shrugged and said they had gone or returned from assignments.

"Assignments for what?" I had asked.

"To do things that need doing," she'd told me. "Like that

floor over there that needs sweeping."

I hummed a ditty Angus had played for us to help with our learning process, then grabbed a scrub brush and worked the bottom of a pot that looked like someone had cooked the beef stew an hour too long.

I was almost panting by the time I finally dug deep enough to reach the bottom of the slimy gunk inside the pot.

"Darn it, now I have that song stuck in my head, too," Clem said as she wrestled with a cast-iron skillet. She dipped it into a sink filled with sudsy water and pulled it out again for more.

"Angus *did* say that learning it via song helps us retain the knowledge," I answered. "Then he started talking about the human brain-something or other, and I spaced out."

"Well yeah, you attach anything to music that annoying, and you'll never forget it," Clem said.

"You'll have nobody to blame if you get to test day and draw a blank. All you have to do is hum all the songs that you have stuck in your head, and you're golden." I looked up from my pot and smiled.

Clementine shuddered as she put a deep fryer basket up to dry and picked up a bunch of dirty cooking knives. "But that means that we'll have to have Angus's creepy singing voice playing on repeat in our heads. I can't imagine a worse punishment. People will beg to be sent to the mining colonies after about an hour of that."

We both laughed.

"Chatty ones, these new girls, wouldn't you say?" asked a voice from the back of the kitchen. "Damn pretty, though."

I hadn't even heard anyone enter the room, but there were a couple of boys standing in the opposite corner of the kitchen. One, a shorter blond, was leaning against the wall. The other, heavier and taller than his friend, was sitting on one of the counters. He had a knife in one hand and a piece of fruit in the other.

Both looked like they were in their late teens. The black-haired boy seemed like he was almost old enough to be an adult, but I couldn't be sure.

"Just ignore them," Clem said, shaking her head and digging back into the dirty skillet.

"Boy, ain't that the truth, Alonso," the blond one said, tucking his pad into a pocket and leaning closer to the counter that his friend was sitting on. "You two sure are beautiful. What are your names? I'm Bart. This is Alonso."

Clementine rolled her eyes.

"Nice to meet you girls," Alonso answered. "I gotta tell you, I bet you both could use a break from all this cleaning, huh? Maybe spend a few hours with a couple of guys like us. We could show you a better time than this."

"No, thanks," said Clementine.

"Aw, come on," Bart said, frowning. "You ought to thank us for being so nice to you. This place ain't made for girls as pretty as you two. We can protect you. Maybe bring you back something nice whenever we're out."

"That's right," Alonso said, walking up to Clementine. I could almost feel his eyes on her whole body, and it sent goosebumps down my back. "I bet it's hard staying inside all day, doing chores. We've heard about you two. Heard you can't leave."

"Your skin looks so soft and pretty," Bart said, getting close to me. "Has anyone ever told you that before?"

I felt like something sank down into my stomach, making me sick, making my hands cold even though they were under the steaming water.

"I didn't think so," Bart continued. "I bet no one ever tells you nice things like that."

Alphonse smirked. "If you ask me, you're the prettier one," he told Clementine, but she didn't seem to react. "Your butt is way better than hers, and that dark hair makes your eyes really pop."

"Go away," Clementine muttered.

"Huh?" Bart asked. "Are you listening to us? We're paying you a compliment. That's no way to treat a guy who's being nice to you."

"We didn't ask you to be nice to us," Clem said.

"So what?" Alphonse asked with a gruff. He placed his hand on her shoulder, swinging her around. He was a head taller than Clem, towering over both of us. He ran a finger across her bangs, moving them out of her eyes. "Don't you like it when a guy does that?"

She stared at him, a firm look on her face, totally devoid of any fear. "Not really," she said.

He snickered. "We both know that's not true."

I dropped the brush, pressing my fingers into the dirty bottom of the pot, trying to stop them from shaking. This feeling was too familiar, too fresh and horrifying.

My mind started wandering, jumping elsewhere. Mother making walnut and chocolate cookies, wrapping me up in her arms and telling me that everything was going to be alright.

It was getting easier and easier to slip into that daydream.

Bart touched my waist, and I felt my throat tighten. "I bet you'd like to get out of here, huh?" he asked me. "Alonso, maybe we can take them to our room."

"Good idea," he answered.

I kept ignoring them, but it was getting increasingly difficult.

Clementine turned away from Alonso, saying nothing. She seemed to be handling it better than me. She just kept on scrubbing that skillet, taking the time to clean deep into the grooves where grease had accumulated. I wished I could be that calm.

"Playing hard to get, eh?" asked Alonso. "I bet you drop that act when I get you in my room."

"Miss Pearl told us to get these dishes clean," said Clem, her voice totally relaxed and casual, as though this was all so routine and simple. As if these two boys weren't about to do something terrible to both of us. "If you don't mind, that's exactly what I'd like to get back to. You wouldn't want to get on Miss Pearl's bad side, would you?"

I looked over at Alonso, who laughed when he saw my face. I wondered if he could tell how scared I was right now. He had that same hungry look that Mackavoy had back at the orphanage when she sat me on that couch.

Alonso leaned over Clem's shoulder, his annoyance starting to show. "Come on, let's get out of here. I'll treat you the way you should be treated. I'll give you a real good show, too. I know you want it. No one else is going to be this nice to you."

I caught him looking back at me. I found my brush buried deep in the sudsy water and gripped it tightly.

Out of the corner of my eye, I could see Clementine smiling as she dipped the skillet back into the steaming water. "That's a very generous offer, Alonso," she said, her voice soft and sweet as she kept her hands in the water. "But I'm afraid I'm going to have to decline. As I said, Miss Pearl will be angry if we don't do our jobs."

Alonso laughed again, but this time, it felt forced, like he was trying to control himself. "Okay, sweetheart, let's go. Bart and I only have about twenty minutes before we've gotta be somewhere, so I wanna make this quick. We can play games later."

He grabbed her arm, squeezing it tightly. I gripped my brush, turning towards him. It was probably better than just my bare fists, but my hands were shaking so much I wasn't sure I could do anything right now.

Maybe I could get the soap in his eyes. Maybe distract him long enough to get away.

My heart hammered inside my ribcage like a rabbit trying to get out.

Something in Clem's hand glinted in the light. It looked vaguely like a cheese knife, but I couldn't see it well enough under the water.

Alonso leaned in closer, bringing his lips to the side of Clem's neck. "You act like a bitch, but you just need a good man to teach you," he whispered. "I'll do that for you. It'll be a favor. You can pay me back later. Don't worry. I can show you how to be a good little—"

Clem swept around to face him with a swift, single motion, burying a knife in Alonso's shoulder. All of this before anyone could react.

It took Alonso a split second to realize what had happened as the force of the blade caused him to stagger back. His eyes fell in shock as he spotted the metal in his flesh, and he let out a terrible scream. It was so loud it hurt my ears.

Clem said nothing.

He opened his mouth, but didn't say anything, and then took a step towards her. She shoved him back, and even though he was bigger, he lost his balance and stumbled into the nearby counter.

Clem backed away, gripping my hand and tugging me towards the door.

"Y-you bitch!" Alonso shouted, his voice cracking. "Get back here! Y-you fucking bitch! Bart, stop them! Don't let them leave."

His friend moved to us, but I kept my eyes down. Still, I could sense his feet as he neared the exit, coming to an abrupt stop. Right then, he let out a surprised gasp as I finally pulling my eyes away from the floor.

Clem halted, forcing me to do the same.

A familiar laugh filled the room.

"Mr. Pryar!" Bart exclaimed, stepping away from the husky, middle-aged man.

Mulberry with his heavy coat and a wry smile, appeared

more amused than anything. Bart and Alonso, for their part, looked absolutely terrified.

I hadn't even heard the man come through the door.

Mulberry shook his head. "I have to say, Alonso, I'm really disappointed in you. Absalom had such high hopes for you, putting all that time and work into your training, and here I see you treating these girls this way. What the hell is wrong with you?"

"I was just trying to be nice to them," Alonso muttered, his eyes twitching towards where the curved cheese knife was still buried in his shoulder. "Sh-she's just crazy. I-I was being nice to her! Wasn't I, Bart?"

"It's true, sir!" exclaimed Bart. "We both were just being nice."

Mulberry narrowed his eyes on them. "If you think I'm fool enough to believe that, then you must not think much of me. Is that it, boys? You think I'm a fool?"

Alonso went red but said nothing.

Bart moved away from Mulberry as the man's face changed to something more dangerous.

"It's a shame," Mulberry said, his voice an even, monotonous grumble. "I'll need to come up with a punishment for this. What do you think, Clementine? Do you have any ideas?"

Clementine pulled her glove off and tossed it away in

disgust. "Mr. Pryar, I—"

"Yes, I guess it'll have to fit the crime, won't it?" he asked. "I could just beat the shit out of you boys myself, but it seems Clementine's already done that part for me. How about six months cleaning this kitchen? You can show these girls how sorry you are by doing their work for them."

"B-but, sir, what about our other assignments?" asked Bart.

"You'll still have to do those, too," Mulberry said. "I hope you can survive on five hours of sleep a night because you'll be working the rest of the time." Mulberry's eyes drifted to Clem. ""I'll be speaking to you later, Clementine. Why don't you two girls go to your room while the rest of us have ourselves a *talk*?"

We both nodded, slipping out of the room as he continued to stare at the two boys, a vacant, passive look in his eyes.

We walked swiftly and quietly out of the kitchen and straight for our room, shutting the door and locking it behind us.

FIVE

I threw my cleaning gloves away and sat on my bed, suddenly feeling tired. I just wanted to close my eyes and settle into my daydream where the people like Mackavoy, Alonso, and Bart didn't exist. I wanted to fall asleep thinking of being someplace else.

My hands were still shaking. The cold feeling had subsided, but the sick remained, sticking to the back of my throat.

Clementine looked angry. She had chewed up the floor of our room, pacing back and forth in the narrow space between the two beds stomping her anger out. It couldn't have been more than fifteen minutes, but it felt like hours.

"Did you hear him?" Clementine tried to make an impression of Mulberry with a growl. "'Go to your room.' Like we did something wrong. They started it, not us. Why the hell are we the ones being punished?"

I didn't look Clementine in the eye. "Well, I mean, we were cleaning, and now we're not. Isn't that better?"

Clem huffed. "Please. Mulberry needed time to check on his

prize boys first. He sent us to our room, so he can scold us for hurting the wittle bitty babies." She made a crude gesture with her finger at the door. "He's going to lay into us, I promise. We're new here, so he'll probably just try to get rid of us. Maybe send us away to work in one of the factories. And if that's how they're going to treat us, I don't want to stay anyway. If the people here are like Alonso, I don't want any part of them."

I nodded, slowly. "Yeah, but did you really need to stab him?"

"Are you crazy?" she asked, spinning around to face me on my bed. "Of course I had to stab him. He *deserved* it. Hell, he's lucky that's *all* I stabbed. Besides, it was just a little scratch. He'll be fine."

Her eyes drifted away from mine, towards the door, and her mouth dropped. I turned around to see both Pearl and Mulberry standing before us.

Pearl looked at her pad. "I wouldn't call a five-centimeter-deep wound to a vital muscle in the shoulder *just a little scratch*. He'll need surgery to repair the damage done to the muscle, and he may have trouble with mobility for the rest of his life."

Clementine stiffened, her face twisting into a less hostile, but still firm expression. "I-I thought the door was—"

"Locked?" asked Mulberry. He raised his hand to show a small key card. "You ought to pay attention more when you're ranting. We were standing here for at least ten seconds before you noticed. And before that, I could hear you in the hall."

Clementine was silent, but I could tell by her eyes that she was trying to find a way out of this. "What are you going to do with us? Are you kicking us out? That's it, isn't it?"

I stepped beside her, taking her hand in mine. If they were going to punish her for what had happened, I was going, too.

Mulberry looked at me, and it made that cold feeling return to my stomach. I held Clem's hand tighter.

"I was only defending myself," Clem said, firmly.

A few tense moments passed as the two of them studied us.

Finally, Mulberry turned to Pearl, his look softening. "She's not wrong."

"You were there," Clem said, raising her voice. It cracked at the last word. "Why didn't you stop them?"

Mulberry tilted his head, letting the question linger a while before he finally answered. When he did, he seemed relaxed, almost sympathetic. "I wanted to see how you would handle yourself. I could've stepped in before things got out of hand, but as it turns out, I didn't need to. Only the weak rely on others to save them, and if I thought you were weak, I would have done so."

Clem tensed, and I felt it. That wasn't the answer she wanted, but it felt honest. "You--" She paused, her eyes darting.

"You should've done something. They had no right to do what they--"

"I know," Mulberry said. He stared at her with a calm expression. There was no anger in him, not like there was with Clementine. "One day, I think you'll understand why sometimes it's better to let people fight for themselves. You might hate me for this today, but it's what you needed. Both of you."

She said nothing, but, I knew those eyes, and I knew her. She would not forget this. She never forgot anything. Even if she grew quiet and appeared to move on, she would always remember. Whether she chose to blame those boys or Mulberry was something I simply couldn't know.

But I hoped she saw the good in what the old man had tried to do.

Pearl relaxed, sighing deeply as she looked at the two of us. "What to do with you now, I wonder?"

Mulberry came closer, eyeing Clementine and crossing his arms. She stared up at him boldly, not shying away from his gaze. My hand trembled in hers, and she gave it a reassuring squeeze.

After what felt like forever, Mulberry nodded. "You were sloppy with that knife, Clementine. I can teach you to be better. Stronger. Would you like that?"

Clem's brow furrowed. "What do you mean?"

Pearl said nothing.

Mulberry continued. "You're green, inexperienced, but we can work with that. It won't be easy. You'll have to train your body as well as your mind. It'll take everything in you...and maybe a little more. Are you up for that?"

Clementine's jaw tightened as she stood before him, her eyes narrowing to match his. "I can do it."

Mulberry raised a hand. "Keep in mind, kid, if you join up for this, you'll be treated like an adult. No more coddling."

I wanted to ask when the coddling had occurred, because so far since we arrived at this place, it had been anything but pleasant. Instead, I only watched as Clem turned the idea over in her head.

She brushed her hands across her cheek and nodded. "If you can teach me to be strong, then I want to learn. I'll do anything you ask me to. Anything."

Mulberry chuckled. "All right, kid. You start tomorrow morning, an hour before the usual wake-up time."

The two adults exchanged a quick glance, then turned towards the door.

My heart was racing. I felt the urge to pull back, to retract from the situation. My body wanted me to say nothing, but I knew I couldn't. I knew I had to do what was best for both my sister and me. "M-Mr. Pryar?" I asked, stepping forward as they crossed into the hall.

He pulled back to see me. "Yes, Abigail?"

I cleared my throat, not because I had to, but because I wanted the extra moment to breath. "I want to join, too."

He tilted his head and stared at me, but there was less shock than I had expected from him. Less surprise. "Why?" he asked, a soft tone in his voice. It was so very different from the way he'd spoken to Clem.

Clementine squeezed my hand. If I looked back at her now, I wouldn't be able to go through with it. I also knew that I wasn't strong enough to survive in this world on my own. I needed her a lot more than she needed me. Hopefully, this training, whatever it was, would change that.

"Because I need it," I whispered. It was a simple answer and an honest one. I just hoped that he wouldn't see how true it was.

But the look in Mulberry's eyes told me that he did.

He turned to Pearl, an unspoken question in his eyes. Her answer was a simple shrug, and she stepped out of the room.

When he turned back to me, he frowned, and I sensed a kind of sadness in him. "Are you sure you want this?"

All I could do was nod.

His eyes lingered on mine for a time, but then his expression hardened back into the man I knew. "Very well, then," he said, giving me a nod. He looked at Clem and again at me. "I'll see you both first thing tomorrow."

SIX

"Again, godsdammit!"

My arms felt rattled and numb with each strike. Pearl said that this sensation would pass as my muscles and bones adjust to the impacts, growing denser, but after a month of this kind of training, I still didn't feel any difference.

Then again, the rubber training dummy was taking the worst of the beating. He was shuddering and shaking with every blow.

I went through the last series again, putting my arms up the way that Pearl had shown me, bouncing lightly on the balls of my feet as I came in closer, throwing my fists at the dummy's face. My shoulders ached with each impact, and as I ducked, I struggled to keep my balance.

Pearl was having none of it. "One foot in front of the other. Abigail, that's not how you make a fist! Do it the way I told you. Clementine, you're kicking too high! Balance yourself, or you'll fall from a godsdamn breeze. Keep going!"

She had transformed into something new, a far cry from

the bored woman we'd encountered before. Here, she was in her element. She was engaged, watching and studying each move, calling us on it, and forcing us to improve.

I was thankful but also exhausted. The day had stretched longer than any we'd spent cleaning. This was a new kind of work, a new kind of life, and it would take time to adjust.

"Once more, Abigail," she said in an even voice.

"Yes, ma'am," I gasped.

I raised my arms again, taking the stance she'd shown us only once. I started with a jab from my left side.

My punches slammed into the gelatinous face on the dummy. The life-sized toy was made to imitate the density of human skin, muscle, and bone. I felt the impact all the way through my knuckles and into my wrist.

And it hurt.

I repeated the move again, ducking under an imaginary haymaker, then gave an uppercut with my right hand. I tried for a mid-height kick to the ribs but slipped and fell to the floor.

Pearl said nothing as I regained myself.

"Sorry," I said, taking heavy breaths. I looked at her, expecting a fierce reprisal for my failure. Instead, her eyes were steady, no hint of anger or disappointment.

"Don't apologize, Abigail. Just learn and adapt," she said. She reached into a nearby container and retrieved a bottle of water, then tossed it towards me. It rolled into my thigh. "Never throw a kick unless you're absolutely sure that you have the balance to complete it. It's better to hold off on the attack than to fall flat on your back. You lose your balance, you die. Do you think you can remember that?"

I nodded, swallowing a mouthful of water and setting the bottle down near the edge of the matt.

"Take a few minutes. We'll try again soon," she said.

I nodded and leaned down on my knees, feeling my sweaty hair drape across my face. It used to be long. I used to be proud of it—my pretty blonde locks. They used to turn gold in the sun.

But Pearl had cut it, saying that long hair was going to hamper my training. In the four weeks since we'd cut it, time had regrown it enough so that I had annoying bangs that got in my eyes every five seconds.

I took another gulp of water, coughing as a few drops went down the wrong pipe.

Clementine was a lot more enthusiastic and energetic about the training than I was. Mulberry had, after all, chosen her first, and now I could see why. I'd just tagged along. I was slowing the training regimen down, but hopefully not by too much.

But Clem was far ahead of me, rarely tiring, hardly messing up. She had a natural composure to her, as though she'd been waiting her entire life for this.

Whatever *this* was. Honestly, I still didn't know.

She worked a series of punches—jabs and uppercuts—and then she hammered an elbow into the dummy's jaw. With a jumping step back, she spun on her back foot and landed a beautiful high kick that knocked the dummy to the floor.

"Nice work, Clementine," Pearl said, handing her a bottle once the dummy was on its feet. "Take a break."

"Thanks, Miss Pearl," she said with a bright grin, tossing her now short black hair and tilting her head to drink some water.

When Pearl walked away, Clem turned and jogged over to where I had taken a seat on one of the nearby stools. "You okay, Abby?"

I was still panting, wiping the sweat from my face with a towel. "Not really. I'm starting to wonder if I should even be here."

Clem's eyes narrowed as she took another sip of her water. "What do you mean?"

I shrugged. "I knew it was going to be difficult, but this is harder than I expected, and with you—" I paused.

"With me what?" she asked.

Did Clem not see how much better than me she was? I shook my head. "It's nothing. I'm just a bit tired is all."

Clem laughed. "Me too. But I feel better through all this, you know? Like, tired but a good kind of tired, I guess. You know what I'm talking about?"

I didn't, but I put on a smile anyway. "Yeah, of course."

"Break's over girls," Pearl said. "Let's get back to it. I want you two to stick closer together from now on. Abigail, I want you studying Clementine's form."

A furious shade of red covered my face, but I nodded. Truth was, I could stand to learn a thing or two from Clem.

We brought the dummies that we were working on closer together and started going through the different combinations that Pearl had taught us all over again.

"Abigail," Pearl called after I finally managed a mid-height kick without falling on my ass, even though the dummy barely moved when I kicked it. "Keep your knees bent and your center of gravity low. It'll give you more power to work with."

"Yes, Miss Pearl," I said, doing as she instructed.

My thighs, already burning from the exercise, screamed in agony as I worked through the series again. This time, when I finished the combination with a kick, the rubber man moved, almost tipping over from the blow.

"What did I tell you?" Pearl asked, and as I looked at her, I noticed a small smile that quickly disappeared. "Now run it again. I want that dummy on its ass before we finish things up today."

I nodded, tightening the wraps on my hands.

When we next took a break, I couldn't help but feel a little frustrated.

I'd kept my knees bent and my center of gravity low, but I still didn't get as close to knocking the dummy over as I had that first time.

If anything, I was just getting worse, and I told Pearl as much.

She chuckled and handed me a bottle and a towel. "You're thinking about it too much. The point of repeating these combinations over and over again is to let your muscles get used to the moves so that when you actually have to use them in combat, your body remembers what it's supposed to do. It's called muscle memory, and it's essential. When you can act without thinking, you'll stand the better chance at living through the fight."

Clementine came over to us, taking a long swig from her water bottle as she flipped her towel over her shoulder. "If you don't mind my asking, how do you know all this, Miss Pearl? I mean, you seem better at this than running us through cleaning this place, but you still haven't told us what you actually do. Have you ever killed anybody? Have you used these skills?"

Pearl chuckled softly, turning to Clem and rolling her neck. "You're a lot less perceptive than I had you pegged for, Clementine. You've been here for over a month now, and you still don't know what it is we're training you for? What do you think it is that we do here?"

I shrugged, even though the question wasn't directed at

me. "I thought you were some sort of security service. Protecting people, helping the innocent."

Pearl smiled at me like I'd just said something adorable and then turned back toward Clementine. "Yes, I kill people. Because aside from keeping the two of you out of trouble, that's precisely what my job entails. I went through a similar training regimen as I'm giving you, though I was a lot younger when I started."

I looked down. I knew that this was the most likely explanation for what they did, but I still hoped it was something else. Something nicer, closer to what the sisters did. Mable obviously knew Mulberry, so she probably knew what it was that he did for a living.

Hell, from the way they had spoken to each other, I was starting to wonder if Mable was a killer like Miss Pearl.

No, I just couldn't imagine it. Mable was the image of peace and patience in my mind, not killing people. It just didn't make sense.

Maybe that was why Mulberry had second thoughts about me being a part of this. I had only joined because I couldn't bear to part with my best and only friend. My selfish decision had put me in a position that I wasn't entirely sure I was comfortable with.

Clementine seemed quite excited by the prospect of our teacher being a trained killer and was bubbling with questions.

"So, have you killed a lot of people? Were they important? Were they bad?"

Pearl shook her head. "I can't talk about the specifics. And you shouldn't ask about them." She paused. "But yes, they were...bad."

"Is that what this whole place is for?" I asked. "Are you training assassins?"

"Yes," Pearl said, simply.

"Is everyone here like you?" asked Clem.

Pearl nodded.

"What's the name of this place?" I asked.

"It doesn't have one," she said.

We both stared at her, confused.

She sighed. "Names are used to identify you. The same is true of an organization, a government, a business. It gives it shape, makes it so you can point to something and understand it. Without a name, you release yourself from the world, fading back into its noise without ever having been seen. Men whisper in fear of the unknown, and that is precisely what we are, simply by existing." She raised a finger, letting silence fill the moment for several seconds, and then continued. "So it is with each of us. When I leave these doors, I become no one. I become shapeless. And when I kill, I do so as a concept, a force of nature."

Clem and I both swallowed.

"Numbers are used as a form of identity, based on our rank inside the organization, but only when communication is needed."

"What's your number?" I asked, timidly.

"Three." Pearl's lips curled. "Mulberry is number one, obviously."

Clementine was looking more and more interested. "Who's number two?"

"None of your business," Pearl scoffed. "Now, it's been more than five minutes, which means it's time to get back to work. I still haven't seen you knock that dummy over, Abigail, and you won't be getting dinner until you do."

* * *

I finally did it. It took most of the afternoon, but I finally managed to kick the dummy off its weighted feet.

The feeling of pride from that didn't put a dent in how tired I felt, though.

My body felt weak with every movement. Even the act of lifting a fork to my mouth got me wondering if I could do this for another day. I couldn't remember ever feeling this tired, and I had been training for a month now.

My fuzzy brain tried to work out that logic. All I could determine was that this was the first time that I had actually applied myself to this. Meanwhile, Clem had been training like this since the first day. She was so fearless, so sincere in her devotion to what we were doing.

I just wanted to keep up.

I didn't bother changing into my night clothes after we got back to our room. I just dropped onto the bed, dressed in the clothes I was wearing. My body felt like it was on fire as my sore muscles burned in agony. But as tired as I was, I still couldn't fall asleep. My brain wouldn't shut down.

I looked up at the ceiling, reimagining the day's routine again in my mind, visualizing all of my mistakes.

"Hey, Abby?" I turned my head to see Clem lying on her stomach, chin resting on her forearms as she faced me.

"Yeah?" I asked, still not moving.

"What are you thinking about? You're just staring at nothing."

So, she'd noticed it too.

It made me smile, giving me enough energy to turn my body on the bed to face her. "Just thinking about Mable. She knew Mulberry very well, and it made me wonder if she was an assassin like Pearl. What if she was number two?"

Clem shrugged and didn't answer, giving me the impression that it hadn't been what was on her mind. So, I asked, "What are you thinking about?"

She paused before answering. "I'm just thinking what my number's going to be."

"It's based on your rank, isn't it?" I asked.

She nodded. "Which means it can change."

"What number do you want?" I asked.

She turned over on the bed, facing up at the ceiling like I had been. "Number one. I want to be the greatest assassin in the universe."

My eyes narrowed.

She continued. "I'll be better than everyone else. Better than Mulberry. Better than Rose and Pearl. All of them. Everyone will talk about the girl with the black hair who doesn't have a name. I'll be a ghost, but I'll be the best."

"Is that really what you want?" I asked.

She looked at me with sheer determination in her eyes. "More than anything in the entire galaxy."

I watched her for a moment, not knowing fully what to say. I only knew that this was important to her, and because I loved her, I had to support it. "Then that's what you'll be, Clem. I know it."

She smiled at the last part and laid back down. "Me too."

I could tell Clem had changed since we first began these lessons. She'd become more determined, more purposeful in her actions. When she went to the training room to practice, she pushed herself to her absolute limit. Even her grades had improved.

Maybe she had always wanted this life. Maybe I'd been blind to this side of her. I couldn't really say.

All I knew was I was afraid. Not for myself, but for her, because the path she'd chosen would be a dangerous one. We weren't in the orphanage anymore. I knew things now, more than I ever had, and one of them was that the world was full of corruption and danger, and it was constantly trying to change you.

Then again, I wasn't so sure the world had done this to her. Not entirely.

Even in our first week here, she'd pushed her boundaries with Pearl. Now that she knew that she could be an assassin, she seemed exhilarated. Not changed, exactly, but completed.

Was she going to keep changing? Keep going down this path? I turned to look at Clem, but she had turned over to face the wall.

No matter what she ended up doing, she was going to be my sister through all of it. Clem wasn't going to change that much, and even if she did, I would always be there for her. I would always look after her, the same way she had for me.

She was my sister, my friend, my partner. Whatever happened after this, we would always be together.

SEVEN

Blinking a drop of sweat away from my eye, I jumped lightly from foot to foot, weaving a bit in place. I bent my knees slightly, moving easily and quickly as I saw a black glove arcing around towards my face.

I ducked under it, pushing forward with my left foot to counterattack. My left hand delivered a probing jab as my right fist hooked underneath, heading for the ribs.

Clementine evaded, bringing her elbow down to block the hook. Even as she dodged, she was closing in. Her left foot darted forward to stomp mine.

I stepped back to avoid it, and she pressed her advantage, feigning with her fist, but then hooking with her other one. I leaned to avoid it, and she clasped both hands behind my neck, holding me there in the clinch and backing me up.

The full weight of her body pressed on me, helped by the substantial strength of her core muscles. She dragged my head down, and her knee came up. My hands caught her knee and pushed it down before it could hit me in the face.

It wouldn't break anything, but it would still hurt like a whore's ass on a busy night, as Pearl was fond of saying.

We continued exchanging blows, blocking most of them, until Clementine finally managed to come in close and wrap her arm around me, bringing our hips together. I tried to break free, but she held firm and tight, leaning to her side and pulling me into the air before slamming me to the floor with a hard hip throw. My back hit the mat with a loud smack, surprising me.

She pretended to stomp at my neck, ending the match.

"You're getting better," she said with a grin.

I scowled up at her, making an annoyed sound as I gripped her hand and got to my feet. "Is that why you almost pulled my arm off and took it home with you?"

She laughed. "You never know when you'll need a spare."

I stuck my tongue out at her as we grabbed our water bottles and towels.

"You need to stop charging at openings like a blind masoon, Abby," Clem said, referencing the large animals we'd recently read about in class. They slept sixteen hours a day, but if you woke them, they'd chase until they fell over from exhaustion, which could strangely take up to several days. They also had tunnel vision and hated the color yellow. "That's twice in one fight. All I had to do was wait for you to drop your guard, which always happens if I'm patient enough."

I nodded, stripping the padded gloves from my hand and the guards from my face. I filled my mouth with water and after swishing it around a few times, spit into the floor drain behind us.

Clementine made a face. "Gross," she said, still undoing the padding from her knuckles.

I grinned. "Just washing the taste of defeat out of my mouth."

She shook her head. "Come on, you weren't that bad."

"Neither were you," I said.

We both laughed.

The gym door opened, and I turned to see Mulberry enter. He looked like a fairly well-to-do businessman out for a night of fun. Clem's face reflected my own confusion, but before we could say anything, Pearl shouted, "You two! On your feet!"

We'd been here for three years now, and Pearl had taken to simple observation, with only the occasional correction as the two of us sparred with one another.

She and Mulberry were already talking by the time we jogged over to join them.

"Rose couldn't handle it," Mulberry said. "She mucked it up big time and got herself flagged at Customs. Thankfully, the target still doesn't know that we're coming for him, so he hasn't upped his security yet. It's easy, but there's still a time issue."

Pearl rolled her eyes as we came closer. "Are you pawning

off another job on me?"

He nodded. "Sure am, because it was your job in the first place, and I only gave it to Rose when you decided to pass on it. We lost our shot at this target, but he's landed in our lap again, and I just can't stand to pass up the opportunity."

"You're talking about three years ago," she said with a scoff. "You can't blame me for that. I didn't want to lose the contract, but it couldn't be helped."

Mulberry tilted his head, almost conceding to her. "Doesn't matter. He's back on our radar and the contract is double the old price. I need this done, Pearl, and I need it done *tonight*. It's the best shot we'll have at him, and we don't know how long the security's going to be this lax. He could go underground, the same way he did the last time we tried."

Pearl let out a long sigh. "Fine. I'll take care of it." She turned to us, her displeasure still showing. "I'm going into the city. It shouldn't take long. A couple of hours at most. I want you both in practicing for the next two hours, and then you'll clean everything up, and—"

"Actually," Mulberry interjected, scratching at the bristle on his chin. "This might be a good opportunity for them to get some supervised field experience. Don't you think so?"

Pearl made a face as she swung around to look at the man. "What?"

Mulberry kept his face straight. "Lax security, in and out in a couple of hours. We couldn't ask for a better mission. Besides, they'll only be observing. You'll be on a rooftop, firing at a distance. Easy training."

"Easy, he tells me," she said, looking at Clem and me. "This is the same contract we lost three years ago because he disappeared, but now you think I should take the girls?" Pearl sighed again.

Before she could continue, Clem stepped in with an excited expression on her face. "We could really use the experience! Right, Abby?" She nudged me with an elbow, and I nodded quickly in response.

Pearl eyed the two of us for a long couple of seconds, her whole body stiff until finally, she relaxed. "Fine," Pearl eventually said. "But if either of you screws this up, it'll be years before you get a second chance at this. Am I understood?"

"Yes, ma'am!" we both snapped.

Mulberry grinned at her and winked at us. "Have a good time, girls. Don't stay out too late." He turned around, pulling the doors open, and exited the training room.

Pearl casually started walking to the exit. "We'll be leaving in half an hour. I want to see both of you showered, changed, and waiting for me at the shuttle exit in twenty. If you're late, you get left behind."

"Yes, ma'am!" Clementine said, running ahead of me to the lockers. It was the most excited I'd seen her in weeks.

EIGHT

Clementine slowed down enough for me to catch up with her, and we stepped inside the shuttle bay together. A handful of transports waited beside a road leading out of the building. It wasn't an expansive area. The room was about as large as our training gym. Like everything else about this place, it didn't even have a name and remained low key and understated. If you were driving by this place in the middle of the afternoon, you'd never suspect it housed one of the most successful assassin guilds in six star systems.

Clementine checked her watch as we entered. "Seventeen minutes and forty-five seconds," she announced proudly. "That's got to be some kind of record for getting ready."

Pearl's voice came from behind us. "Absolutely. You can expect medals and a call from the governor any minute now."

Pearl wasn't wearing training clothes. Instead, she had on what looked like a pure black jumpsuit, black boots, and gloves. It looked loose and baggy, but as she came closer, I saw that the space between the clothes was actually firm and hard, indicating some kind of light body armor underneath.

Clem was immediately interested, reaching out to touch the arm of the jumpsuit.

"Is that Neuro-Mass?" I asked, narrowing my eyes, trying to remember the name. I'd heard of it before in one of my books. Over the past three years, our standard education had been supplemented with a handful of extra courses specifically related to—well, what we were about to do.

One course had covered all the known forms of body armor, both modern and ancient. Neuro-Mass was a type of protection recently developed for the Union's special forces. It incorporated a tactile sensation, allowing the armor to feel almost like a part of the user's body.

Pearl chuckled and shook her head. "No, Mass sets off all kinds of alarms and attracts the kind of attention that I could do without. This has a ceramic-titanium weave underneath that acts like regular clothes until it's hit with something. The impact causes it to harden and stop the attack. It can stave off most small-arms fire, knives, and even blunt-force trauma. If anything gets through, the material releases a gel anti-toxin and coagulant into the wound. It can't stop the heavier stuff, but it's effective in most fights. A bit low tech, but it gets the job done."

Clementine was still stroking the material in pure fascination. "It's amazing. When do we get armor like this?"

An odd smile crossed Pearl's features. "When you're older and ready to have jobs of your own."

I could read the excitement on my sister's face as we headed toward one of the waiting shuttles. Soon, we were heading to the city.

* * *

"You got the mission briefs on your pads," Pearl said. "Read them back to me."

I turned my eyes away from the edge of the rooftop. We weren't in the nicest part of town, but the view from this high up was still incredible. We were near the docks, and I could feel the ocean salt in the breeze as it cut through my clothes.

Clementine had her pad out before me, and she started reading the brief. "Target's name is Michael Dunn."

I narrowed my eyes. Why did that name sound familiar?

Clementine kept going. "Longtime operative and high-ranking official of the Osiris-based drug cartel known as the Conference. He was originally a Union naval officer before being dishonorably discharged when he was caught using his position aboard the *UFS Peaceful Resolute* to smuggle weapons, drugs, and...miscellaneous?"

"Artifacts, electronics, pretty much anything that can be moved for a lot of money," Pearl explained, pulling out the briefcase she brought and putting it on top of a ledge.

I read over the information on my pad. "His wife divorced him after the discharge. The criminal charges were dropped, though. I wonder why."

"Maybe he had the right connections," Clem said.

Pearl nodded, pulling a red velvet blanket from the case, and placing it on the ledge beside the briefcase. "The intel says he was working with the Conference at the time. He funneled military secrets to them for a fee. They slicked a few palms to get him out and the files sealed."

"If they're sealed, how did we get them?" I asked.

Pearl raised her eye like the answer should be obvious. After a moment, she continued. "Once he was released, he started working for the organization full time here in Ruto City."

I glanced down at the pad and continued reading. "He didn't have any kids, and most of his family is dead. He has an uncle living here in the city, though. He has a history of disorderly conduct and possession of controlled substances. No job to speak of, and he hasn't paid any taxes in almost a decade. He's a drunk and a junkie. Dunn has been paying for the guy's housing in this neighborhood."

Pearl nodded again as she started placing pieces of what looked like a rifle on the blanket and putting them together. "Just across the street from this building, as a matter of fact." She fit everything together in under a minute. Lower receiver, upper receiver, bolt carrier assembly, and the rail attachment for the scope. "He's been giving his uncle rent money for the past five years. It appears his uncle has been using the money on drugs and alcohol, though. The target has been informed of this, and after a handful of warnings, he's finally going to make an appearance in person to talk it over."

Clem looked up from studying how Pearl was putting the rifle together, a confused look on her face. "How do we know all this?"

Pearl looked up from what she was doing. "This has been a long-running operation. Dunn has a lot of professionals on his security staff, so we had to have someone infiltrate the organization to get the intel on him. Over the past three years, our operative has been gathering information. She finally found out about the uncle, a possible weak spot in our man's security, and found out that the man was using the money that was being sent for drugs. There's no love lost between Dunn and his uncle, and it seems that Dunn only helps the man out of a sense of familial duty, so our operative leaked the information to Dunn about how his money was being spent. Dunn intercepted the messages, but unfortunately, our operative's cover was compromised in the process. So, we needed a fresh face to finish the job."

Pearl spoke like she'd memorized a script. She pulled a magazine from the case and started fitting rounds into it. "That's me, a fresh face. And you girls are along for the ride."

Once the magazine was full to a capacity of five rounds, she picked up the almost completely assembled rifle and looked through the scope.

Clementine seemed anxious for the job to start, and she moved over to the edge of the roof, looking at the building where Dunn would be visiting his uncle. "So, how are we going to do it?" she asked finally. "Are those bullets tipped with poison? Are they tracker enabled so you don't actually have to be in sight of the building when you shoot it?"

Pearle pulled away from the scope to give her an odd look. "Tracker enabled bullets are pure science fiction. And we don't need poison-tipped bullets when regular bullets are deadly enough on their own." She finished fiddling with the scope, placed the rifle on a tripod, and picked the magazine up again. "Dunn appears to be a bit ashamed of his uncle's habits, or maybe he's cautious since it's a weak point in his otherwise rather impressive defenses. He's coming here without any of his usual security. We can't hit him in the car, which will be bulletproof, and the building has an underground parking garage, so we can't catch him between the car and the building. He'll be coming up to the apartment, though, and the apartment has a broad window that exposes the whole living area. It gives us a clean shot, maybe sixty meters from here, so it won't be difficult, even through the glass.

I'll have to anticipate that he'll be wearing body armor, so I have to shoot for his head."

I nodded, taking all of this in and jotting notes on my pad. This was what we were here for, experience. We needed this if we were going to survive in this business. That was how I had to describe it to myself—a business.

We were dealing with a man's life here. A drug dealer, sure, but a man just the same. A person with dreams, hopes, aspirations, and fears. And Miss Pearl was talking about how she had to shoot him in the head because he probably had body armor.

I sighed. Clementine was full of questions about what was coming next, but I couldn't hear her. There was a rushing sound in my ears, and I just needed to take a moment to pull myself together.

I had been training for this for the past three years, and I knew that this part of the job was coming, but it still didn't make it any easier. I moved over to the other side of the roof, away from Clementine's questioning about the rifle and leaned on the ledge, looking out over the city.

I faced the docks now, with only a couple of smaller buildings between me and a fantastic view of the sun setting over the ocean. The wind flowed through my short hair, making me close my eyes and inhale the briny scent. It was relaxing, and for a moment, I could pretend that the hum of the city around me was actually the sound of waves crashing on a beach somewhere.

I had never been to a beach in real life, but a couple of the holos I'd seen gave me a decent idea of what it was like.

One day, I hoped to visit a real beach in person. I would have a book to read, and I'd enjoy the sun, wind, and the sound of the ocean, all without having to worry about training, killing, or hurting people.

"Target's arrived," Pearl said, snapping me out of my reverie.

I jogged over to where Pearl and Clem were waiting. Clem gave me a pair of binoculars, and I looked across the street. Nothing was happening.

"The target's already in the underground parking garage," Pearl said. "He should be moving toward the elevator now." She peered into her scope. She counted softly under her breath as she looked through it.

"Which window are we looking at?" I asked, scanning the apartments in the building opposite us. Pearl pressed a button on her scope, and a highlight marker appeared in my binoculars, drawing my attention to a window on the twelfth floor, three windows to the left of the fire escape.

Pearl kept counting as we stared through the window, watching and waiting until a light came on. A man dressed only in a pair of briefs stepped into our line of vision. Despite the hour, it looked like he had just woken up. He was skeletally thin, to the point I could count his ribs, and he had massive dark rings under his eyes.

"Methamphetamines?" I asked. We'd learned about the various side effects of popular recreational drugs during our alternative lessons. Dunn's uncle fit the textbook look of a meth head.

"Among other things," Pearl muttered and went back to counting.

The semi-naked man reached the apartment's door and examined the video feed to see who was outside. He clenched his fists and glanced around anxiously, almost like he was searching for somewhere to run. Finally, his shoulders slumped, defeated, and he unlocked the door. It was halfway open when Michael Dunn shoved it open the rest of the way and shouldered past his uncle.

Dunn wore an expensive three-piece suit, matching his file's description to a tee except for a weak goatee on his chin.

Now that the target was in sight, Pearl stopped counting and readied the next round in the rifle, dragging the bolt back with a soft click. She used caseless ammunition, eliminating the need for cleanup. There were only the bullet and the propellant—the latter disappearing in a puff of smoke and the former going far away. They were expensive and illegal, but so was the business of killing.

I looked back at the apartment across the street, and another man walked through the door. While also dressed in a suit, his was cheaper looking, like a uniform. He wore sunglasses, and a black earpiece looped behind his ear.

"Looks like Dunn brought security," Clementine said, adjusting her own binoculars slightly.

"Is that a problem?" I asked.

"Not really," Pearl said. Her voice was distant like she wasn't really there. "Possibly a complication but not a problem."

I nodded, pretending I understood the difference between the two. I didn't ask because Pearl was concentrating, and I didn't want to distract her.

Dunn looked visibly angry, and his uncle groveled in front of him, cowering and skittish like a beaten dog. He probably needed a fix.

"Clem, you're my spotter," Pearl said, pressing the butt of the rifle up against her shoulder and taking a long, slow breath. "Give me the rundown."

"Yes, ma'am," Clementine answered, looking into her binoculars a bit more closely. "Target is sixty-five meters away, with a twelve-meter drop. Wind shows at three kilometers per hour, eastward."

Clem seemed to be going over a mental checklist. When it came to calling a shot, the closer you were, the less this type of information mattered. A sixty-meter shot didn't need to take into account air pressure and altitude.

Clem finally finished and leaned into her binoculars again. "Fire when ready."

The arguing in the apartment had reached a fever pitch, with Dunn looking like he was going to blow a vein in his forehead. His face was red and furious. His uncle's head hung low, and he made apologetic gestures with his hands. The security guy seemed intent on staring at the door for the entire conversation, his face expressionless.

He seemed collected and professional, but he missed the looming threat from the nearby rooftop. I wondered if it would cost him his life.

Pearl took a breath and released it. As soon as her lungs were empty, she squeezed the trigger. The kick was minimal. It wasn't a powerful rifle. Pearl didn't need heavy artillery for a shot at this distance. She was using sub-sonic rounds, and the suppressor that elongated the barrel by about twenty centimeters was allowed to do its job.

The noise still sounded distinctly like a gunshot, but it was quieter by about fifty decibels. The window shattering on the other side of the street was louder.

Dunn's head snapped back, a red dot appearing between his eyes, and the wall behind him was suddenly sprayed with blood and brains. His body went limp, and he fell.

"Target down," Clementine said, sounding excited.

Pearl adjusted the angle of the rifle on the tripod, picking out the uncle as a second target, and squeezed the trigger again.

Despite his ragged appearance, Dunn's uncle was quick to get on the floor, ducking behind a sofa and crawling quickly out of sight.

The security guy jumped into action, drawing a weapon of his own and aiming it at the window. His mouth was moving, apparently calling the situation into whoever was on the other end of his comm.

"We should go," Pearl said, pulling the rifle away from the ledge before the man could see it. She spread the red blanket on the rooftop and placed the gun on it. She took it apart in quick, practiced motions. Clementine and I ducked behind the ledge, too.

"That was amazing," Clem said with a broad grin.

"It wasn't that difficult," Pearl said, meaning the shot.

Dunn's uncle called for help. His voice carried over to our rooftop perch through the ruined window. I heard other people screaming. I assumed they were neighbors who'd heard the gunshots. Law enforcement or peacekeepers were probably on their way, and I wondered how a drug cartel might react to that.

Pearl stowed the rifle parts away and shut the case, clicking it closed and locking it. She turned to us, already headed for the door to the stairwell.

"A quick escape is always essential," she said as she walked. "Whenever you're on a job like this, it always pays to have at least three escape routes planned beforehand. In our case, it won't take the security guy long to figure out where the shots came from, and he'll be sending officers our way any minute. If we're lucky."

"And if we're not?" Clem asked, something like giddy excitement in her voice as we reached the stairs.

"He'll be sending whoever hired him to run security for a high-ranking member of a drug cartel." Pearl turned to us as we started heading down the stairs. "I think you can imagine which is worse."

I could. I had seen pictures of what cartels did to people when they wanted to send a message. Things got ugly when they had a reason to get violent.

I'd take six months in a corrections cell, personally.

Twelve flights of stairs were easier going down than up, and we reached the bottom in minutes. As we exited the building, police vehicle sirens alerted us that they were on their way. They were still at least six blocks away, though, since I couldn't see any flashing lights. The dread of being caught made me sick to my stomach, but to my relief, Pearl didn't let us have much time to think about it.

Her pace looked natural, but Clem and I almost had to jog to keep up with her as we walked away from the building that would be swarming with cops and other questionable characters in a few minutes. Pearl didn't look too worried.

She looked more relaxed than she had since we started. She turned quickly into an alleyway off the street. Once we were out of sight, she started jogging, heading deeper into the alley.

She found a door at the back of the alley and unlocked it. It opened without the creaking that I would have expected from a rusty old door.

We entered a department store storage area, full of hundreds of clothes racks, mostly still wrapped in plastic. Pearl stripped off her jacket and gloves in a hurry, keeping only her jumpsuit and boots as she pulled a new jacket from one of the racks. Once she tore the plastic off and put it on, she pulled a couple more off their hooks and handed them to us.

"Always be prepared," she said with a wink. "I had these dropped here last night."

I tore the bag open, slipping on a dark blue shirt with a skull on it, along with some black pants. There was also a jacket and a pair of winter gloves, along with a beanie to cover my hair. This was something I never would have worn, but I supposed that was the point.

Once we changed, we followed Pearl to the other side of the room. It opened up into a parking area where the shuttle was waiting, not far from the door.

Less than ten minutes after pulling the trigger, Pearl had us in the air, accelerating towards the other side of town.

NINE

Over the next few days, Clementine was almost impossible to keep up with.

She was full of a manic energy that allowed her to train at a frenzied pace. I knew why she was so driven all of a sudden. Clem had a dream, and our little excursion with Miss Pearl had been a solid step toward realizing it.

She wanted to be the best, most feared assassin in the known universe. I wasn't ashamed to admit that the thought terrified me a little. I hadn't taken this path to be a killer. I just wanted to stay at my sister's side.

Sparring with her was now difficult. Clem dialed up the intensity of our matches and had overcome her previous limits for all of our exercises. Her focus on our regular studies had slightly waned, replaced with a desperate hunger for other forms of knowledge, such as strangulations, poisons, stealth, and geopolitics, not to mention the various criminal organizations where nearly all of our hits came from. She was mostly interested in knives and close-range attacks. I ended up in our room alone most nights, reading my books as she spent more and more time in the gym.

"It's necessary," she told me as we took a break from rock-climbing one afternoon. One of the walls in the gym had been converted into a revolving cliff-face, perfect for full body movement exercises. "If I want to be the best, sacrifices must be made. I have to focus on training, which means that I don't have time for things like math and history. That's how it works."

I furrowed my brow as I patted my hands with chalk powder. "I don't know. I think if you work hard at everything, you can be more well-rounded. The fact that you won't be the best at one doesn't matter because it gives you a wider range of options. Having options makes you less likely to end up in a vulnerable situation. A generalist instead of a specialist."

Clem shrugged, rolling her shoulders as she took a drink of water. "We're assassins. We've got one thing to worry about. Killing. There's no room in my head for pointless garbage like those stories you've been reading."

I blinked, surprised by that. "I—"

"What? You didn't think I noticed you doing that when the lights were out? I knew you weren't studying trigonometry. I'm not stupid." She shook her head. "And I'm not saying you can't read what you want. I'm doing this, so you can have that. It's not for me."

I said nothing.

She jumped up to the first handhold, gripping it firmly as her feet found their place on the rocks, helping her to grip the next and begin the climb. "You coming?" she asked, looking down at me.

"O-oh, sorry," I said, quickly. I took a deep breath and exhaled, then gripped the nearest rock and sprang up.

I was sweating hard once I'd reached the ten-meter mark. I could feel my forearms and shoulders burning from the exertion five meters higher. The sweat dripped down my back, making it difficult to focus as the handholds were getting harder and harder to reach.

Suddenly, as I reached for the last one before the peak, my feet lost their grip, and I dropped from my perch. I only fell a meter before the slack in the rope on my harness caught me.

"You'll get it next time," Clem said with a grin. She waved at me, her hand coated in white powder.

I watched her move easily from hold to hold, and I shook my head in wonder. It all came so naturally to her.

I kept an eye on her harness as she climbed the moving wall, each of the holds continuously moving down. There was no end goal to this, no place you had to reach before it was over. This was an endurance test, and Clem had always outlasted me.

"She's making good time up there," I heard a voice behind

me say. I jumped, startled. It was Pearl, chuckling softly at my surprise as she moved over to the wall. "My best time up this wall is twenty-three minutes, forty-seven seconds. Galion is the best at it. I remember his time was something like forty-eight minutes and change."

I'd met Galion a few times. He was a shorter man with dusky skin, black hair, and almond-shaped eyes. He had been our hand-to-hand combat instructor when Pearl left for two weeks, off on some mission. He was agile, quick, and powerful. It wasn't hard to believe that he'd be able to last so long on this wall.

I looked up to see Clem still moving, a wide grin on her face as she leaped to a hold that was difficult to reach.

I grinned back but couldn't help a twinge of jealousy as I watched her there, twenty meters in the air, acting like it hadn't even been that hard. I supposed for her, it probably wasn't.

"What was my time?" she asked when she was back on the ground.

"Eight minutes, thirty-seven seconds," Pearl said with a smile. "That's a minute longer than the last time. Not bad."

"You beat your best time!" I exclaimed with a smile. "At that rate, you'll be leaving Pearl in the dust in no time."

Pearl chuckled. "Let's not get ahead of ourselves."

I stepped in about to take the strap from Clem to have another try myself, but Pearl stopped me. "We're doing something new today. Follow me."

We both frowned but didn't argue.

She led us through a series of hallways, guiding us into a far spot of the building that was previously off limits to us.

When we entered through the door, Pearl gave us each a pair of protective glasses and earpieces in a gray prep room. She pulled two cases from a shelf, and we followed her to the main room. It was pretty massive, although not quite as wide as the training area we'd just come from, but certainly much longer, like a giant rectangle.

For the moment, we had the whole place to ourselves. Pearl walked us toward the edge of the room and then placed the two cases on separate benches before turning towards us.

"You recognize these, don't you?" she asked, pointing to them.

Clem nodded. "They're what you used to carry your rifle in." She paused. "For our job."

"*My* job," Pearl corrected in a playful tone, but her eyes told me that she wasn't entirely kidding. "Yes, these are the cases that carry disassembled rifles that we use on many of our operations. The casing is meant to be as nonchalant as possible, but I'm sure you're both smart enough to guess that."

She opened each case, revealing the pieces inside, all neatly arranged and ready for assembly. On one side of the case, a red felt blanket was folded up.

"So cool," Clementine said, her eyes gleaming as she studied the disassembled rifle in front of her. "So, are we doing target practice?"

Pearl smirked. "That depends. You'll find manuals inside for how to assemble the rifles. Pay close attention. Eventually, you'll need to learn to put them together and take them apart quickly while in the field, but for now, it's important to learn how to assemble them correctly, so have patience and take your time." She motioned toward the cases. "Begin."

I pulled the blanket out and laid it on the bench like I remembered Pearl doing a couple days ago on a roof. No wrinkles, completely flat across the surface. There were smaller pieces to this puzzle, and I didn't want any of them getting lost.

I pulled out the manual, studying it closely before starting to piece it together. The scope, firing pin, muzzle, and so on. Everything had its place. Still, even with instructions, learning how to build something took time to master, but the more I did this, the faster I would become. It was like any other skill.

After a few moments, I snapped the empty magazine into the rifle, then stood and looked at Pearl. "Done."

Clementine and Pearl both seemed surprised. "You are?" asked Clem.

I nodded. "Think so."

Pearl took the gun and examined it, checking every piece to make certain, and then nodded. "Very good, Abigail." Her eyes drifted to Clem, who was still watching us with a slack jawed expression. "Are you done, too?"

Clementine stiffened and dropped her focus back to her weapon. "Not yet! Almost!"

Pearl handed the weapon back to me. "Take it apart and do it again. You were fast for your first time, but still slow compared to the rest of us. We'll keep doing this until you can both do this in under thirty seconds."

Clem and I sat there assembling and disassembling our weapons for the better part of an hour, trying our best to get faster and more precise. I wasn't sure why, but I actually found myself enjoying this. There was something about the way the pieces came together, something about the smell and the feel of the metal.

Pearl's inspections were quick and thorough each time, causing me to wonder how many she had done before now. Hundreds? Thousands? It had to be as familiar to her as breathing, the way she had been with her own rifle on the roof.

"Nice work," she said after another inspection, handing the rifle back to me. "Come on, both of you. That's enough practice."

We followed her to a bench, where she set the rifle up on the tripod. Pearl pulled a case out of her pocket and withdrew five bullets, placing them on the blanket next to the weapon.

She held one of them up. "These are long-range precision rounds, otherwise known as nexus bolts. They're untraceable, citywide threat scans can't detect them, and they can penetrate four-centimeter-thick glass from three hundred meters away. This is what I used on our job." She looked at Clem with a half-smile. "You're going to practice now, so you can learn how they feel."

"Really?!" asked Clementine, her face lighting up. "Yes!"

"Enough of that," cautioned Pearl, lifting her hand to steady Clem. "Calmness first. Work on that. You can't get excited when you're using these weapons. They're not toys. They're death itself, and you need to learn how to wield them like adults."

"Yes, Ms. Pearl!" said Clem, still full of energy as she forced herself to sit still.

Pearl's face remained calm as she stood over us. "Now, both of you, load your weapons and get ready to fire. We're going to be here for a while, so take your time and get this right."

* * *

I pulled the magazine from its box and quickly slipped the five bullets in, then screwed the suppressor into place, rolling my shoulders as I pulled the rifle closer to me. I heard Pearl pressing a control panel, and a paper target came into view, dangling by some wires. It was near the other side of the long room, too far for me to see the details. I could only make out its shape, which resembled a man.

"Call it," she ordered.

I leaned into the scope, pressing a small button on the side. It activated a laser that coincided with the crosshairs of the scope. It wasn't visible and not used for targeting, but rather for measuring the distance between me and whatever my scope was aiming at. A display appeared, showing the distance.

"Fifty meters," I said, dragging the bolt back and chambering a round.

"Most shooting instructors would tell you to aim for center mass," Pearl said in a soft voice. "But like with Dunn, a lot of the people that you'll be shooting at will be wearing body armor. You'll have to get used to shooting for the head."

I didn't respond, but shifted my shot up a few centimeters, taking long, deep breaths. I felt excited, oddly enough, and I could sense my heartbeat quicken. Was I nervous? Afraid? Intimidated?

No, that wasn't it. This was something different—the same feeling I used to get when Sister Mable told me stories of the outside world. The same feeling I had when I thought about my make-believe parents.

I was having *fun*. Shooting.

A gentle jitter touched my fingers as I leaned into the rifle, feeling the stock press into my shoulder, and I exhaled.

I gently squeezed the trigger.

A loud pop echoed through the room, mostly covered by the earpieces as the rifle jerked against my shoulder. A moment later, I took control again, finding the target with my scope. I had missed the head, but when I looked again, I saw that I hadn't missed the target entirely. There was a hole about ten centimeters down from where I was aiming and a little to the left.

"Well, your target's dead," Pearl said. "But it'll be messy and showy. Carotid artery, lots of blood. Not a clean kill, but not bad for a first shot. Want to try again?"

I nodded, chambering another round and peering down the scope. I felt a bit calmer now. Our education had covered this. I aimed higher and to the right of where I'd shot the last time.

I heard Clem call to Pearl, telling her that she was finished with her rifle now. I didn't pay attention. I was staring down the scope, taking long, slow breaths. Another pop, another jerk into my shoulder, and this time, the hole appeared dead in the center of the target's head.

No comment from Pearl, but a click from the control panel moved the target back another fifty meters. I adjusted my aim and shot again. Another two hits. The first one a little low but still on the head. After those two, she moved it out to the maximum distance of the shooting range, one hundred and fifty meters.

I could hear Clem cursing softly after she took a few shots.

"Squeeze the trigger, don't jerk it," Pearl told her. Clem responded with more unintelligible cursing.

I took a deep breath and shifted my aim up about three centimeters. The jitters were long gone. For the first time in my life outside of a book, I felt in my element, comfortable and at ease.

My heartbeat was even and slow, although I could still feel a gentle tick-tick-tick in my fingertips as I squeezed the trigger again.

But it was good. It was right.

This time, all three shots landed on the head, nearly equal distance from each other, forming a crooked triangle. I looked up from my scope, unable to stop my lips from curling into a stupid grin.

Another click of the controls brought the target buzzing across the range towards us. Clem was already looking at her target after five shots, and the expression on her face was less than pleased.

"A good grouping," Pearl noted while examining mine. She used a pen to mark the spots where my bullets had struck with an X. She wrote the distance down too, taking the time to circle the triangle I had made.

I moved over to check out Clem's paper target, and I saw why she wasn't pleased. Her shots had all been from fifty meters away, and only two had struck the head. A few had hit center mass, another in the neck, but multiple shots were missing altogether.

"It's because I had to take it apart again," Clem explained, scowling. "It ruined the calibrating of the rifle. I would have had it otherwise."

I nodded. "That was probably it. I bet you get way more hits next time."

Clem smiled, reaching out to squeeze my hand. I squeezed back.

* * *

Over the next few hours, Clem *did* manage some improvement, even putting together a neat grouping out at a hundred and fifty meters. She had a problem with the moving targets though, only hitting one of the five through the shoulder.

"Fucking godsdamn piece of shit!" she yelled as her last shot hit the back of the wall, missing all six targets completely. She picked the rifle up off the tripod and threw it on the dusty floor as hard as she could.

My eyes fell on Pearl, wondering how she would react, but she was on her pad, tapping away at what looked like a message.

"You break it, you pay for it, darling," Pearl finally said, putting her pad back in her pocket. "Not that you have any money, but I'm sure we can find some extra chores for you to do."

Clementine looked angrier than I had seen her in a long

time. "It's not my fault that this thing doesn't shoot straight."

The last time she'd been like this, she'd just stuck a knife in Alonso's shoulder.

Pearl remained perfectly calm. "Gun's fine. You just need more practice."

Clem scowled. "I've been practicing."

"For what, three hours?" Pearl shook her head. "You have an affinity for close combat, but that doesn't mean you'll automatically excel at everything you try. Take Abigail here, for example." She motioned at me, and I felt myself blush. "She has a talent for this, with a required patience that many otherwise lack. Learn from her as she has learned from you."

Clem's eyes darted to me, still angry. I thought she was about to lash out at me, but instead, she simply sighed. "Fine," she muttered, bending to pick the rifle back up. She put it on the blanket and started taking it apart. "I'll clean it and try again."

She had to clean dust from some of the pieces, but by the time she was finished and folding the blanket up, Pearl had left and come back with what looked like a thick belt made of leather.

"These aren't really my specialty," Pearl said, laying the belt on the table. "It's more Galion's thing. Talk to him, and he'll teach you how to use them."

Clem leaned in closer to the belt, her hands touching the Velcro strap that kept it closed. Eagerly, she pulled it open, and for a moment, her eyes seemed to gleam.

There was a line of knives inside. Some throwing blades. A fifteen-centimeter-long combat knife. Another that was longer, curving at the edge. There were so many kinds, most of which I'd never seen before. Each of the grips were charcoal black, and the metal a kind of gray. Upon closer inspection, they didn't look fully real.

Clem was utterly entranced. "Are these for me?"

"For your training, yes," Pearl answered with a smile. "Keep them clean and sharp. When you're ready or during one of your training missions, you'll be given real and proper weapons. For now, learn to use these."

"Thank you, Miss Pearl!" Clem exclaimed, already jogging toward the exit.

"Where are you going?" asked Pearl.

"To find Mr. Galion, of course!" she replied. "I want to get started right away!"

When she was gone, I turned back to Pearl. "So, I'm not getting a belt of knives?" I asked.

"No," Pearl said, a smile on her lips as she placed a hand on my shoulder. "I have something else in mind for you."

TEN

My eyes flicked left and right. My heart pounded in my ears, and my stomach tightened.

I had gone over this drill for what felt like a hundred times, but it never failed to lodge my heart in my throat. I blinked a droplet of sweat from my eyes, and my fingers held tightly to the rubber grip of the pistol in my hands.

It was small, easy to conceal, and relatively quiet, made even more so by the ten-centimeter suppressor. The downside was that a gun this small had very little in the way of stopping power. That meant that each shot had to count. I had to be precise.

Pearl had spent the better part of the last three months drilling me in the various advantages and drawbacks of each choice of firearm.

And I had to admit, I liked them all very much.

I brushed my arm across my eyes, wiping the sweat away as I moved slowly. I kept my senses attuned to any sounds around me as I moved toward the corner, careful to control my breathing the way that Pearl had taught me to. It didn't slow my heart rate, but it did keep my hands from shaking.

The training still wasn't easy. I had mixed feelings every time I went to bed, and I kept dreaming about pistols and target dummies, but at this moment, I felt a whisper of a thrill inside my chest, a rush of exhilaration that pulled at me in ways I'd never felt before I learned to hold a gun. A sense of satisfaction came from doing something that I was good at. It was hard, but each solution that I reached felt natural and easier each time.

I took in a deep breath, dropping down into a squat and twisting my body around the nearby corner. I had to hit the targets before they hit me.

As soon as I had one in sight, I squeezed the trigger. The gun kicked lightly back into my hand, and I released two rapid shots with great precision, tagging the dummy as it swung around, bringing its laser towards me. As the red beam landed on the wall beside me, it disappeared, seemingly dead. Another rotating dummy appeared through the leftmost wall, this time knowing my exact position. Smart Targets, Pearl had called them. They learned where I was from my actions, which made things all the more difficult.

Still, I couldn't hear my heartbeat anymore.

I squeezed the trigger again. The small weapon coughed and jumped back in my hands. The new target went still as the bullet slammed into its center red ring, located where the head would be, indicating a kill shot.

Another came from the rear immediately, this one swinging its head and torso, breaking my view of the targets on its body. I brought the barrel to meet the dummy, and immediately fired two quick shots, each at its head.

Hit. Hit. Dead.

The dummy stopped rotating and came to a complete stop, slumping its head and arms forward to simulate death.

Three targets. Three kills.

Clean kills were essential to our work. They kept the organization in demand, high at the top of our clients' call list.

I still wasn't sure how old the organization was. Angus the V.I. always deflected my questions when I asked. Probably Mulberry's fault.

He was also the cause of the extra stress that I had dealt with during this mock-mission. Over the months since our mission with Pearl, Mulberry had come to watch me train. Not all the time, but it was typical to find him watching me once or twice a week. I wasn't sure why he did that, except that he must be trying to decide if I was worth keeping around. I couldn't say I blamed him for that. I was nothing compared to the rest of them.

Pearl, for example, was a real artist with guns. She could hit every target faster than me, and she knew so much about firearms that I found it inspiring. Her mind was like an encyclopedia of death.

"Range is clear," I called behind me.

Pearl entered, squatting down to inspect the dummies. She put a marker on where each shot landed. I moved towards her for a closer look.

"Not bad, Abby," she said, a sense of satisfaction on her face. It was a rare but pleasing thing to see, and I found myself hoping for it every time we did this. "Not bad at all."

I grinned back, doing a small mock-curtsy. "Why, thank you, Miss Pearl."

"Keep in mind, no matter how good the dummies, real people are unpredictable." I heard a deep, rumble of a voice from behind me.

I had learned to anticipate Mulberry's silent approaches. They no longer took me by surprise like they had when I first came to this place. Back then, I could have sworn to the gods that he was actually a ghost, capable of walking through walls.

Perhaps he was, and I had only grown used to it.

"Headshots all around." Mulberry came closer. "You know, I think we may have a budding prodigy on our hands."

"Pearl's a great teacher, Mr. Pryar," I answered. "She could teach anyone to do this."

Pearl cocked her brow and smiled at me, taking a moment to ruffle my hair playfully as she walked past me.

"Keep it going, kid," said Mulberry, giving me a slight nod. "You have a long way to go, but you're getting there."

I smiled and returned the nod. I wanted to ask if Clementine could join me but refrained. The two of us still had class together, as well as general exercise and hand-to-hand combat lessons, but the specialization lessons were taken individually. Pearl was teaching me how to handle a wide selection of firearms, while Clem was undergoing similar instruction in knives and blades of all sorts from Galion.

I had seen him fighting, and I estimated that he had to be Number Four or Five in the guild. I took a few classes from him myself, trying to expand my skill set. While I wasn't at Clementine's level, I could feel myself improving a lot with each session. My confidence was better than it had once been, and it made everything else so much easier.

"Well, it's time for lunch," Mulberry said. "But I want you and Clementine reporting to my office right after. I have something that I need to talk to the two of you about. Understood? Shall we say, an hour from now?"

"Yes, Mr. Pryar," I said, inspecting my pistol and twisting the suppressor off the barrel. "I'll be there."

* * *

"Did he tell you what this was about?" Clementine asked, jogging to catch up with me.

I shook my head. "He just said to be in his office right after lunch. Said he had something he needed to talk to us about."

Clem narrowed her eyes. "What did you do?"

I turned around, surprised. "What? Nothing. I didn't do anything. He just told me—"

"I'm kidding, you idiot," she said with a laugh. She grinned and pressed her fist into my shoulder. "You need to work on not being so gullible."

"I'm not that gullible, I—" I paused, not sure how to continue that argument. "Okay, fine. I'll work on it."

Clem grinned. "Adorable."

It was my turn to playfully punch her in the shoulder, so I did.

The door was open when we arrived, and Mulberry was already seated at his desk, reading over something on his pad. We quietly entered and took our seats opposite him.

"We have a new assignment on Osiris," he started, the low rumble of his voice still unmistakable as he set the pad down on the desk and looked up at us. "A kill order on a member of one of the criminal factions here in Ruto."

So, this was another job. We'd gone with Pearl on fourteen individual assignments by now. Each time, the work had been easier, smoother, simpler than before. We had done as she'd told us, and slowly we were able to take more responsibility. Never any kills, though. We both still had yet to pull the actual trigger ourselves. I suspected that time would come eventually, although I wasn't looking forward to it.

"Why isn't Pearl here for this?" asked Clementine, and I suddenly realized she was right. Pearl had always been in the room during a mission brief.

"She's not going with you this time," he said, plainly.

The two of us paused, blinking curiously at the old man before everything finally clicked.

"Are you saying—" Clementine paused, excitement bubbling up in her expression. "Are you saying this is ours?"

He nodded.

I raised my brow. I could see Clementine almost jumping out of her seat, only stopping herself by gripping the arms of the chair.

"I—we're ready, Mr. Pryar!" she said, grinning.

Again, I found myself caught up in my sister's excitement, smiling despite the growing dread in my stomach.

A job of our own? I couldn't fathom the idea. We'd improved in our training, been on a handful of missions, but we weren't experts yet. Far from it, actually.

"That's what Pearl and Galion have been telling me, Clementine, but I'll still be joining the two of you on this assignment. There's a fantastic little sandwich shop right in the area that makes the best meatball subs this side of Epsy, I swear to gods." He looked longingly into the air above us like he was picturing the food.

It made sense, I supposed. Our first assignment would have to be supervised, but it only made the knot in my stomach worse. If I failed, it would be under Mulberry's eye.

His smile disappeared as he picked his pad up, flicking the screen towards the left wall, which carried the image from the device and blew it up tenfold.

"The target's name is Jodie Crom," said Mulberry, right as the man's face appeared, along with a series of details regarding his appearance and some key info about his past. He was a pudgy looking man with pale skin, a receding hairline, and what looked like a lazy eye. "He's a front-runner for a smuggling ring that deals mostly in weapons here on the planet. He's been known to trade in other areas, including drugs and sex trafficking. Over the last few years, he's grown his wealth as well as his belly, and it's made him slow and clumsy. I thought he'd an easy way to break the two of you in."

I studied the man's face, but also Clem's. There was something manic in her eyes, the look of storm clouds brewing. She looked confident. Determined. I was glad for that because it meant we wouldn't fail.

"The research for the job's already been done," Mulberry

continued, running through a series of stills of Crom's house, with marked notes for entry and exit. A handful of suggestions in handwriting that I recognized.

Not everyone in the organization was an assassin. A lot of them were security specialists whose job was to plan out the operations, finding points of entry and available exits, weak spots in security, and to make any suggestions to allow for a seamless and smooth operation.

Mulberry clicked the screen back to a picture of Jodie Crom. "Our target has some breathing difficulties, as well as high cholesterol. Introducing a very common cholesterol medication known for constricting the airways via aerosol form will make for the smoothest kill. Normally, you'd only take a small amount of it per day, but we're giving a heavy dose of concentrate, which should suffocate the target while he sleeps. Undetectable. Untraceable." Mulberry leaned back in his seat, studying us. "However, since you two will be the boots on the ground, you may need to adapt and come up with an alternative, should things go south."

Clementine couldn't stop herself this time, jumping lightly to her feet. "You can count on us!"

He smiled. "I know. Now, for your first job, we'll be providing you with suits." He tapped a small screen embedded in his desk. "Pearl, are you here with the equipment yet?"

The door opened, and Pearl came in with a couple of full-body jumpsuits in her hands. I tried to look into her eyes, but she avoided my gaze as she placed the suits on the table and left without saying a word.

Clem and I both stared as she left. I wondered what was wrong? Was she mad at us? It was always hard to tell with Pearl.

"These are top of the line," Mulberry said, pulling our attention back to the equipment. "The same kind of light body armor that is standard for our Operatives. The surface is a matte black. So long as you stay in the shadows, you'll be out of sight. It also blocks infrared and radar, as well as having a temperature regulator so it will shield you from heat scans. Even so, it doesn't always work against the more sophisticated security systems, so you should still be careful. Remember your training. Don't rely too heavily on technology. Machines and fancy suits are great, but at the end of the day, your own skills are what will keep you alive. The rest of the details will be transferred to your pads. Get your suits on, and report to the shuttle bay in thirty minutes."

ELEVEN

I sat in the back of the shuttle, tugging at the uniform. I was supposed to look like the service staff of the building we were infiltrating, but I felt silly. The outfit fit me to perfection, slightly baggy to accommodate the body armor underneath.

Running my finger over it, I could feel the armor slightly adjusting to my movements, adapting to protect my body.

I'd get used to both the armor and the service outfit soon, I decided, and leaned back in my seat.

It was odd to think that when I woke up this morning and pictured what I'd be doing this evening, it had been something entirely different. Since I didn't have any other classes, I'd hoped to catch up on a book I was reading. It was called *SmokeBarrel*, a story about a female Renegade who had found herself stranded in a small desert town. She'd taken a contract to pay for repairs on her ship, but the job had led to a surprising series of events that would ultimately lead her to take down a powerful warlord. The Renegade's name was Shelly Connors, and she had a certain way of speaking that I found admirable. Brash and brave, forward and direct. She was never afraid to tell someone how she felt about them.

It was easy to escape into a world where I wasn't the one having to fight all the fights. Where someone who should, by all standards, be the villain, but would so often chose to do the right thing.

"Hey, are you listening to me?"

I looked up, blinking and focusing back on what was in my hand. It was the pad with the information on the target. I had zoned out while reading it and had even flipped a few pages down without thinking. "Oh, I'm sorry," I said to Clem, blinking. "I guess I'm a little nervous."

"Come on," she said, smacking my knee. I felt the armor react to the touch. "This is it. This is where we prove ourselves and show everyone that we're ready to be part of the team. Can't you be a little excited?"

I looked away from the pad, trying and failing to fake the emotion she wanted to see.

She placed a hand on my shoulder. "You're not scared, are you?"

I shrugged. "Not scared," I lied. "It's just, the anticipation is getting to me."

Her arms wrapped around my neck in a warm hug. "We're going to rock this, you and me. Just keep that in mind, and we'll do fine."

I nodded. She was right. Whatever was bothering me didn't seem to have the same effect on Clem. She could do this job well enough for both of us.

Mulberry's voice boomed from the front of the shuttle. "Fear or anticipation for the task ahead is something that everyone feels." I felt a flush run over my cheeks, embarrassed that he'd heard our conversation. "No matter how experienced. It's adrenaline, getting your body ready for what's to come. You'll get used to it. Learn to control it and make it your strength."

"Hey, boss," Clem called to Mulberry. "When do we get our numbers?"

"This job formally initiates you into the organization," Mulberry said. "Once it's finished, you'll be assigned individual numbers for field use. Until then, over the radio, I'll just call you Raven and Sparrow."

"Am I Raven?" Clem asked.

"You're the one with black hair," he answered. "What do you think?"

"So, I'm Sparrow?" I asked. "I like that."

The shuttle came to a stop. Mulberry unstrapped himself from the driver's seat and came back, handing Clementine a small bag.

"This is an exit bag. Has Pearl explained these to you

before?" he asked.

We both nodded. Exit bags were used for suicide, at least most of the time, but could be used as a silent attack as well. The bags had the benefit of being an inert, untraceable gas that was already naturally present in the atmosphere, wouldn't cause an alarm response in the target while they slept, and guaranteed death in a way that would seem reasonable to a coroner as consistent with the risks of certain medications, of which this man took many.

"We'll handle it," Clem said with confidence. She took the bag and tucked it inside her suit.

Mulberry nodded. "The kill will be fast and simple. He'll be in his room, sleeping next to his latest woman. Clementine will take the kill. Abigail, I want you on lookout."

We both nodded.

Mulberry pulled out a key card and handed it to me. "You need to be in and out before anybody realizes that the target is dead. Keep an eye on the exits and find the escape routes. If you run into security, take care of them and keep moving. Never stay in one place for longer than thirty seconds. That key card will get you past the lobby and up to the target's floor. I'll be down here, and you can contact me over the comms. Remember to not call each other by name while inside, and only call me *Comm*." He placed a hand on each of our shoulders, an intense look in his eyes.

"Good luck."

We stepped out of the back of the shuttle, pulling on long trench coats to cover our suits and gear. The target lived in a fifty-story luxury apartment building.

There were cameras and security, but both were made with the interest of protecting the privacy of the wealthy inhabitants.

"Nervous, Sparrow?" Clementine asked me.

"Excited, Raven," I answered in a deadpan voice.

My eyes were already studying the outside of the building. I gulped, trying to hide my apprehension, and then the two of us walked toward the building.

      * * *

We reached an unguarded side entrance, far from the main lobby.

There was a moment of panic as the card processed, then relief hit me as the light blinked green, and the magnetic lock released the door.

The first area appeared to be a laundry room, but none of the machines were running, and no one was around. "Looks like everyone's gone for the night," said Clem.

The comm in my ear clicked to life. "We chose tonight because it's a holiday," said Mulberry. "The building has a skeleton crew. Security is a different story. Check the third dryer nearest to you. Number sixteen. It has two packs of clothes inside. Find them now and remember the location for later."

Clem popped the lid on the dryer and pulled out two bags, each marked with a blue label. We'd gotten used to the drill by now, having done this with Pearl so many times.

She shoved them back inside and tapped her ear. "Got them."

"Now, bring up the map of the building and work your way to the target," explained Mulberry.

We reached the elevator, and I pressed the card into a second sensor. This one reacted immediately, probably lacking the kind of security programs the first one had. A screen came to life, showing an image of the building and a message: "Seventeenth floor: Confirm?"

I pressed the green button, and the doors closed, slowly taking us up to the seventeenth floor. I looked down at my suit, which was covered by the coat. *It still looks wrong*, I thought as I pulled on a pair of thin, black gloves and drew my pistol from its holster under my shoulder.

"You any good with that?" Clem asked, checking the pack with the canister.

"I'm not bad." I pulled the slide back to load a round into the chamber and flipped the safety off, making sure that the suppressor was fitted tight. "Are you any good with those?" I asked, eyeing her knives.

Clem grinned, lacking any kind of modesty as she drew a pair of knives from their sheaths. "One of the best, I've been told."

I returned her smile.

Despite the jokes, I could sense the anticipation in my body begin to rise. It was always like this. Jittery before the action, but focused when it started.

I had a fifteen-centimeter combat knife tucked into a sheath strapped to my right thigh, as well as three extra magazines for the pistol. If I needed more beyond that, we already failed.

Clem, for her part, had brought a belt of knives and nothing more. I wondered if that had been Galion's recommendation.

A soft ping signaled our arrival. I rolled my neck and pulled on a mask to cover my face, then raised the pistol as the door opened while Clem also slipped on her mask.

The elevator opened right into the target's apartment. It was one of the most lavish places I'd ever seen, steeped in glimmering glass on every wall, fine furniture with velvet cloth, and a sparkling chandelier hanging over the dining room table. Soft, evening lights illuminated the inner hallways, lending the apartment a dreamlike quality.

I licked my suddenly dry lips and covered the living and dining rooms quickly before gesturing to Clem that it was clear.

The target's bedroom wasn't much farther.

I checked my pad with my free hand. Odd. No motion or heat sensors. Maybe they only relied on the security down in the lobby.

I tucked the thought in the back of my mind for later as Clem waved for me to keep going.

We reached the other side, and she leaned in close to me. "The brief says that the security teams for each floor have a pretty impressive response time. So, we can't let the target's wife hit the panic button or scream, I guess until we're already clear."

I nodded as I scanned our surroundings, keeping my stance low and tightening my grip on the pistol. The second floor had a balcony that looked over the first. It led directly into a hallway with a couple of doors branching out to the right and to the left. According to surveillance, the target would be in a bedroom about twenty paces down the hall at the end of the fork.

"How big is this place?" I whispered as we moved down the hall, keeping my voice low and my senses on high alert.

Clem stepped in behind me and slightly to my left. "I'd rather know how expensive it is to live here. If you had all this money, wouldn't you leave this city? It's a shithole."

I shrugged. We had been living rent-free in the complex for the entirety of our training, and more than a few of the already established operatives had their own individual rooms. I'd never cared much for fancy things or high-rise buildings.

Honestly, I'd never considered where I'd live after we left the guild. Between the orphanage and this, I'd never had to think about it. I shook the thought from my mind. Now was the time to focus on the task at hand.

We reached the fork, and I glanced down both sides before giving Clem the all-clear. The left-hand hallway had a single door leading to the master bedroom, where our target would be sleeping. I moved towards it, gingerly reaching for the antique gold door handle, and twisting it. Despite its apparent age, it was perfectly oiled and turned without making a sound.

The door swung open silently.

I realized I was holding my breath and exhaled slowly. There wasn't much light in the room, but I noticed two figures on the bed—one covered, the other not. The uncovered figure was a man, sleeping completely in the nude, snoring gently.

He appeared to match the description of our target, but we'd have to move closer to verify.

I motioned with my head for Clementine to go in while I kept watch. She moved slowly towards the bed, stepping lightly over the carpeted floor as I peeked out the door. There was no sign that our entrance had been noticed. Yet.

The guy was rich, and he was a criminal, yet he still slept in his own bed every night, right next to someone he cared about.

Most of my assumptions about the people in this kind of business, with these kinds of resources, led me to think of numerous infidelities. Maybe that was true of him. Maybe not. Maybe this was the love of his life.

Even for criminals, true love was bound to happen.

I turned back to watch Clementine, who had made her way over to the bed. She took out the exit bag and quietly stood there, waiting.

Her eyes fixated on the sleeping criminal, watching his chest heave in the dark. The mask hid her expression, except for her eyes, which seemed to narrow in contemplation momentarily. After a few seconds, she took the canister and placed it back in her waist pocket.

What was she doing? Was the act of killing him too much for her? I couldn't blame her for that. Neither of us had ever done something like this, so it made sense to be afraid. I wanted to reach out to her, to touch her arm and tell her not to worry. Maybe we just weren't ready for—

Clementine pulled a long, wickedly curved knife from her belt, bringing it above the man in the bed. It gleamed in the light from the window, reflecting off the nearby wall.

I stiffened, opening my mouth to ask what the hell she was doing, but I didn't dare make a sound. Not even a whisper.

I shook my head, waving a hand at her to grab her

attention, but she didn't respond. I took a step closer to her, hoping to draw her focus away from the target and back to me. If I could just talk to her, figure out what she was thinking, maybe we could—

Clem plunged the knife into the man with a meaty slash. The man's eyes bulged open. Blood spurted over the bed sheets as he desperately tried to inhale. A lungful of blood made breathing impossible, and he let out a loud, strangled garble.

The woman woke up immediately. Her eyes turned towards Clem, who leaped on top of the man and straddled his waist. She pulled the knife back out of him and plunged it once more into his shoulder, then into his neck, and repeated the process three more times. With a swift and final slash, she tore the blade through the target's throat, sending a spray of blood onto the woman beside him.

There could be only one reaction.

The lady screamed. It was the kind of shriek that you heard in horror holos—loud, high-pitched enough to break glass, and more importantly, it carried itself far and wide. The security team would hear it, even through the walls.

We were done.

"Shit," Clem said as she jumped over the target's corpse and reached for the frantic woman, but she had already rolled off the bed.

I circled around, not quite knowing what to do. The woman reached underneath the bedside table, pressing a button just before Clem reached her with the freshly drawn kukri knife, stabbing her in the side of her neck and dragging the blade from end-to-end. Another muted thud followed as the woman hit the floor, blood rinsing out of her like a piece of butchered meat. Clementine scrambled out of the bed and dove towards her, using another knife to slit the woman's throat.

I turned away, anxious and terrified, not to mention, absolutely sick to my stomach.

"What the fuck are you doing?" I asked, turned away from the scene.

Clem didn't respond. She simply looked towards the door I was supposed to be guarding. "Listen!" she snapped, motioning with her bloodied knife to the hall.

Footsteps and voices were growing steadily closer.

"Time to go!" I snapped.

Clem nodded, and we fled into the nearby hall. The dining room came into view, the glistening chandelier sparkling above us. Not far to the elevator from here. We just had to—

A heavyset man came charging from another corridor. Clem leaped clear of his path, but I wasn't fast enough. He slamming directly into me, shoving me into the nearby table. I slid across it, rolling across the middle of the floor until I hit the wall.

Even though it all happened before I could process it, the suit absorbed most of the damage. I pushed myself on my side, locating the thick man with padded armor on his chest. He had a tattoo on his neck, although I couldn't make it out in the dark, and a metallic, prosthetic arm. Based on how hard he'd hit me, the arm made sense.

I retrieved my pistol, but he was too fast. The gun left my hand as his foot slammed into my fingers. While nothing broke, I still screamed.

He raised his metal arm again, but I dodged, kicking at his face in a desperate attempt to keep him away. Suddenly, Clem charged him, sticking one of her knives into his shoulder.

He reacted by swinging his arm around and hitting her in the stomach.

The force knocked her into the nearby kitchen but gave me enough time to move away from him. As he turned his attention on me again, I frantically searched for anything to use as a weapon. A lamp. That's all I could—

I grabbed hold of the bar and yanked the cord from the wall, hitting the guard with the base of it, directly in his shin. He cursed, and I feared it had only made him angrier.

"Hey!" shouted Clem.

We both turned to the kitchen nook where she stood at the counter with a set of kitchen knives.

They flew at him, one after the next, and he managed to block the first few with his arm, but had to move to avoid the rest. Even with the armor, Clem's throws were deadly. He was smart to avoid—

A butcher knife flew between us, colliding with the man's knee with such force that it stuck.

I found my gun in the chaos, then got to my feet.

The man raised his metal arm towards me, and it began to morph into something else. A barrel at the end.

"Sparrow!" cried Clem, coming back from the kitchen in a full sprint.

She dove onto the guard's neck, stabbing his shoulder with her knife just in time to send his bullet into the wall beside me.

I ran close, leaping over his arm and digging the pistol into his neck.

I fired, splitting his throat on both sides.

Clem backed off, and I shot him again in the temple, finally causing him to go limp.

We were both heaving, breathing hard enough that it burned. "Gods," I muttered.

"What's going on in there?" called Mulberry over the comm. "Is the target eliminated?"

"Confirmed," said Clem, holding the nearby wall as she tried to catch her breath.

"Then I want you gone. Get to the laundry department and—"

Two men appeared from the hall behind us. In the heat of the moment, I'd forgotten to watch my surroundings. One of them rushed me, but I reacted at once, sidestepping the attack.

The world seemed to slow as he went to grab me, and I responded automatically, bringing my pistol to his chest and firing. Centimeters from his ribs, the gun sent the bullet all the way through, and he fell away from me, dead before he hit the floor.

The bright flash blinded me from staring directly at the gun when it went off, and I dropped the weapon in surprise.

Clem's yell registered over the ringing in my ears, and she jumped nimbly beside me, charging at the second man. A knife in her hand flicked toward his neck. He evaded the knife and grabbed Clem by the neck with his uninjured hand. Stopping her in her tracks, he paused briefly with an ugly smile, then lifted her off the floor with a single hand.

"No!" I snapped.

I jumped forward, forgetting my gun on the floor, and drew the knife from its sheath on my thigh. The monster tracked my movements, but Clem tossed her knife into her other hand and stabbed it firmly into his bicep.

He roared but kept his grip on her neck.

I circled around, my heart hammering at seeing Clem being suspended like that. Her face was already turning a dangerous shade of purple. I jumped on top of the man from behind, tangling my legs around his torso and wrapping my free hand around his neck.

He reached back for me, and I quickly stabbed him in the shoulder. The wound didn't slow him down. He grabbed the top of my head and tried to dislodge me, so I dug the knife into him again. And again. And again, punching the short, broad blade through the thick muscles in his neck. I was trying to find his carotid artery, but in the middle of so much muscle, I had a hard time of it.

Warm blood splattered my mask and coated my arm while the man's grip on me loosened. He finally dropped Clem as she fell to her knees gasping for air and clutching her throat. I dropped down as the man staggered forward, trying in vain to staunch the wounds, but collapsing before taking more than three steps.

My eyes were on Clem. I wiped the knife clean on my sleeve before sheathing it and running over to my sister's side. She pulled her mask up to breathe freely but coughed as soon as it was off. I knelt beside her and placed a hand on her shoulder.

"You okay, Cl—Raven?" I asked.

She didn't answer, only nodding as she struggled to her feet and pulled the mask back down.

My earpiece buzzed as Mulberry's trademark growl filtered through it. "I just intercepted a call to the local authorities about someone triggering a silent alarm. I suggest you leave. *Now*. Do you hear me, Sparrow? Raven?"

"Yes, sir," I answered, then gestured for Clem to follow me. I swept my gun up from the floor on my way out, while Clem picked up her throwing knife.

I sprinted for the end of the hall, skidding to a halt and spinning around once I reached the elevator. Clem was right at my heels as I entered the lift. My throat felt dry, my hands sweaty inside my gloves, but I tried to keep a cool head.

What would Pearl do?

The light above the elevator blinked, indicating that it was on its way to us. "We're about to have company," muttered Clem, placing her back to the wall beside the lift doors.

I positioned myself on the adjacent side, giving my pistol one last check before the elevator opened. "Raven, I—" I paused, trying not to panic. It took everything in me to stay calm. "Maybe we should try another way. Didn't the plans show an emergency exit?"

Clem hesitated. "The alarm will sound if we go that way."

"That's good," I said, grabbing her wrist. "We can use it as a distraction. Come on! We took those other guys down, but we can't handle an entire team."

She blinked, processing everything. "R-right. You're right."

I brought up the building schematics and pulled her with me, heading to the far end of the hall and around the end corner, straight into a closed set of doors. We both looked at one another, then shoved the silver handles inward, causing the overhead lights to come on and the alarm to sound.

"Emergency! Emergency!" stated the automated system. "Evacuation protocols initiated. Remain calm and proceed to the nearest exit."

"Let's go!" I shouted, yanking Clem's hand through the opening and into the stairwell. We shuffled down to the next floor, leaping two or three steps at a time, trying to outpace the residents from the other floors. As soon as my feet hit the bottom level, I peered up to see almost every single door open, filling the stairs with shuffling footsteps as the building's residents arrived.

We were both breathing heavily, our black suits obscuring the red blood that coated us. I quickly checked my gun, opting to replace the magazine before continuing.

I had been through hundreds of training sessions, and while it wasn't exactly the same, I had gone from feeling overly anxious to focused. Somehow, all of that training had worked, and I'd found myself ready.

I could do this. I could be an assassin.

A short corridor later we found the laundry room. As we

had with Pearl on the first mission, we exchanged our outfits with the blue-marked bags in the dryer and got dressed quickly.

I tossed on my fresh shirt, pants, and jacket. Clem did the same. I pulled the mask off my face, placing it inside my suit's leg compartment. It was still wet with blood and sweat.

We packed our old clothes into the same dryer and started through the same door we'd entered when we first arrived, heading into the back alleyway and towards the eastern street.

The crowd had already gathered there, filling the entire area with a bustling mob of confused people. Children cried in their parents' arms, while others complained loud enough to be equally distracting.

Several police vehicles lined the street, shining lights that mimicked a circus show. I stepped into the mob, staying quiet and trying not to bump into anyone. Clem followed, saying nothing.

When we were safely on the other side, I fled into the park, getting behind a set of thick trees. Our pace quickened from there, and we raced to Mulberry's shuttle.

"We did it!" Clem yelled, skipping instead of running.

"We're not out of it yet," I said.

Clem rolled her eyes. "I know we're not," she said, although now she was whispering. "But we got the target, and we're out of the building." She giggled, genuinely satisfied.

Mulberry's shuttle was at the same place we'd left it. The

doors opened, and we jumped inside with the engines already primed and ready. As we lifted off the ground, Mulberry stepped hard on the accelerator, and we quickly careened away from the building.

"What the hell happened in there?" Mulberry asked, looking back at us as his growl turning into something closer to a roar.

He had a dangerous look in his eyes, almost murderous.

"The target was awake and, on his feet, when we got to the room," Clem said before I could answer. "Might have been going for a piss or something. We had to act, but we woke up the wife."

Mulberry's eyes shifted over to me for confirmation.

I hesitated.

Clem's eyes were on me too, so I sighed. "H-he saw us," I said, nearly vomiting out the words. "I moved deeper into the room than I should have. That's why I wasn't covering the door."

Clem grinned and turned back to Mulberry. "We took care of it, though. Got every single one of them. You should've seen us, Number One. We were out of this world!"

TWELVE

Getting used to a regular schedule the next day was going to be difficult.

My face had swelled up during our getaway from where the giant had clipped me. I had to spend hours with a cold pack to get it back down to something resembling normal again. In the heat of the moment, I had taken more bumps and scrapes than I had noticed and was feeling achy and painful all over.

My ears were still ringing from the unsilenced shots, and it was painful to move after I had gone to bed.

They canceled most of our classes for the next day. Angus only showed up on my pad to pass along a couple of lessons regarding the physics involved in a shot spanning more than one thousand meters. I couldn't bring myself to look at it.

For the first few hours of the day, all I could do was stare up at the ceiling. Exhausted after the mission, I was practically falling asleep on the way back home. My sleep had been dreamless, but when I woke up, the memories of what happened the night before—what I had done—all came back to me in a slow ebb.

First, watching Clementine kill the target herself. I didn't dispute that it needed to be done. We were on the job, and the man was a terrible human being. I would be lying if I thought anybody other than his mother would miss him. No, he wasn't bothering me.

It was Clementine.

There was a desire in her eyes when she moved over him. It hadn't been enough to simply kill the man. She needed to get up close and deliver the killing blow herself, to feel his flesh give way around her blade.

I was hoping I had only imagined the expression on her face. The room was dim, and I'd only had a moment to catch her eyes. Maybe she had intended to do it the right way, but he woke up when she came close. Maybe she had no choice but to use the knife.

Who was I to judge her anyway? I had blood on my hands, too. Did it matter if our target died by gas, knife, or gun? Murder was murder, and I'd done my fair share of it.

It took me most of the morning to come to terms with that. Clementine had been up early, gone before I woke up, so I had the room to myself, allowing a long morning of silent contemplation and self-reflection.

"I wonder what Mable would think if she knew," I said

aloud, reaching up into the air above me and grasping at nothing.

My shoulder ached.

I closed my eyes, but all I could see were the bodyguards' faces. The man charging at me, enraged by the death of his friend. I hadn't seen the big fellow's face as I killed him, but I did remember seeing him holding Clementine by the neck, lifting her off the floor, and then I saw red. It didn't matter to me anymore that he was a human being.

All I knew was that he was hurting my sister, and by every scrap of will in my body, I was going to stop him. It. Whatever.

I rolled over on the bed, reaching underneath and pulling out my book. It was a little worn out. Galion had given it to me, saying that it was one of his favorites. The cover was a bit faded, but it showed a woman in full armor with a gun in her hand, shooting at an unknown enemy. There was a small, scrappy ship, framed with a beautiful view of the sky behind her.

I smiled, running my fingers over the cover.

I found my spot from last time. I usually folded the page where I stopped to make it easier to pick it up the next time I wanted to read, but since it wasn't mine, I didn't want to damage it.

I had to give it back once I finished it of course, but the story made me want to find the rest of the series. There was probably a store in the city that sold hard copies of books. I liked having the physical paper in my hands, reading over the printed letters. It felt more grounded and made it easier to immerse myself in what was happening.

Slipping into the comfort of the pages, I let the day pass me by. I missed lunch. I imagined being in the conflicts the heroine found herself in, sometimes even saying some of her cooler lines aloud.

Clementine thought I was crazy for doing that, but in the end, it was what made the book enjoyable to me. The ability to slip into someone else's skin for a little while, and able to escape my own troubles and live life on the gritty edge, where violence was glorious and always had some sort of deeper meaning.

The hours passed, and I even missed that the sun had set. I only had a few chapters left when Clementine returned. She had just come out of the shower from the looks of her wet hair, but her cheeks were flushed, and she had the distinct look of someone who had just finished a vigorous workout.

"Hey, Abby," she said with a smile. "Have you been in here all day?"

"Yeah," I answered, putting the book down and stretching. Had it really been all day?

"You need to get some exercise in, stretch those limbs. It'll help the bruising heal a lot faster."

I nodded, relaxing against the bed again and looking up at

the ceiling. "I know. But with no classes or anything to get to, I just needed some time to myself."

She looked at me, a confused smile on her face. "What for? We had our first successful job last night. We should be celebrating. I mean, we need to get paid first, but then we should celebrate, right?"

I shrugged. "I don't know. We killed people. I mean, the target was an asshole that deserved it, but what about those guards? Weren't they just doing their jobs? Did they deserve to die too?"

Clem sat down on her bed, a thoughtful look on her face. "Well, it was them or us, wasn't it? I mean, they were just doing their job, but they would have killed us, or worse, sent us to jail. Is that what you'd prefer?"

"Of course not," I said, propping myself up on my elbow. "But it wasn't them or us, was it? If you'd just used the canister like we'd planned, the wife wouldn't have woken up until we were already gone, and none of them would've had to die."

"You can't know that," she snapped, looking annoyed now. "What if the medicine didn't work? He could have built up a resistance, or they might not have put the right concentration in the canister or something. With a knife..." She looked down, and I knew she imagined a knife in her hands right now. "With a knife, you can feel it. You just know. There's no room for error."

I shook my head and laid back down, staring up.

The researchers had done their jobs. They wouldn't have suggested the gas if they weren't sure, and Mulberry had advised us to use it, too. It hadn't been a matter of her doubting the gas's effectiveness. It couldn't have been. I knew that she trusted Mulberry well enough.

So why hadn't she used it?

Clem's face softened as she moved over to my bed and put a hand on my shoulder. "Look, you noticed how I was going on about what a good job I'd done to Mulberry on the way back?"

I looked at her, confused. "Yeah? What about it?"

She squeezed my shoulder gently. "Well, last night, I saw what you're capable of. You're an artist with that gun. It was amazing to watch. Hell, you saved my life when that big fucker had me by the throat. I was feeling insecure. Before then I never realized how good you were, and well, I think I felt threatened. You were amazing last night. Like, proper godsdamn fantastic."

I felt my face grow warm, and a small smile touched my lips. "You saved my life too."

She grinned and brushed her fingers through my short hair. "See? This is what I'm talking about. We've got each other's backs. We're the future of this organization, and together, we're damn near unstoppable."

I placed my hand on her shoulder and grinned. "I certainly

hope so."

"Am I interrupting something?" I looked up to the door where Pearl was standing with an amused expression.

"Just talking about last night is all, Miss Pearl," Clementine said in an upbeat voice.

"Good, because Mulberry wants to talk to you girls about what happened yesterday, too. He wants to see the both of you in his office."

I got up from the bed, groaning as the pain from the bruises intensified from my moving. I could feel my face throbbing. I pressed my hand up, cradling it gently, and we headed to Mulberry's office for the second time in as many days.

* * *

When we arrived, Mulberry was waiting for us, and he quickly motioned for us to take our seats.

"How're you two feeling?" he asked, once we sat down.

"I need some ice," I groaned. "And maybe a few painkillers."

Mulberry grinned and leaned back in his seat. "We'll get to that in a bit. For now, we'll be looking over what happened last night."

I nodded, feeling a lot more somber about it than Clem apparently did. She could barely keep a smile off her face as Mulberry skimmed over something on his pad.

It wasn't hard to tell that Clem had clearly enjoyed herself last night and was looking forward to more. I, on the other hand, felt like I'd gone through a crucible. But it was a career that I had chosen for myself. I had no choice but to keep moving forward.

Mulberry glanced up at us. "Well, I heard back from the client. Even though things didn't go as planned, we're all chalking this up as a success. Even with the collateral damage, the target is down. There doesn't seem to be anything leading back to the client or us. It wasn't perfect, by any means, but it was still a win. Congratulations, you two. You both officially graduated."

I raised my eyebrows. "Graduated?"

"You showed competence in the field, and the ability to improvise on the fly. You need to sharpen your skills a bit more, but that's not going to happen here at the complex. From now on, you're official members of our organization. That means you'll be receiving new assignments, additional access to the armory, and clearance for certain levels of intelligence." Mulberry smiled, but it wasn't a happy smile. Closer to satisfied, but that wasn't quite it, either.

Clementine didn't notice. She leaned forward in her chair. "So, do we get our numbers now?"

"You do, indeed," Mulberry said, leaning forward in his seat and checking his pad. "Clementine, you are now Number Thirty-Six. Abigail, you're Number Thirty-Seven."

Clementine grinned. "Cool!"

"But that's not all. Check your pads. You'll find bank accounts set up in your names, with monthly deposits and additional bonuses when you complete your missions."

I pulled my pad out, and sure enough, there was a bank account with a new transfer for two hundred credits. I checked Clem's, and it said the same.

"Most of the pay went into the creation of your uniforms. But your next job won't have the same expenses, and you can expect some hefty income soon, once you complete the next assignment. You'll be traveling between the neighboring colonies and systems, depending on the job. It's the best business in the world if you've got the stomach for it."

"Thank you, Mr. Pryar!" Clementine said, rising from her chair.

"You can drop the formalities, kid. Just call me Mulberry."

I rose as well but said nothing.

He dismissed us, and the moment the door closed behind us, Clementine punched me in the shoulder. "We did it! We did it!"

"Ow, ow, ow!" I said, genuinely in pain from the night before, but then I feigned a smile, trying to match her excitement. "Yeah, we did it. Great job, Miss Thirty-Six."

"Hell yeah! Now, what do you say we blow our hard-earned cash in the most irresponsible way we can find, Miss Thirty-

Seven?"

I tilted my head, still feeling rather unsettled but decided not to show it. Whatever had happened in that building, and whatever Clem's reasons, I wasn't sure I wanted to talk about them. "I could use some food," I said, trying to shift the conversation. "Can we start there?"

THIRTEEN

I concentrated my eyes on the scope and pressed the rifle snugly against my shoulder.

My first instinct was always to close the eye that wasn't on the scope, but Pearl advised me against it, saying it wasn't a good habit. It takes focus to keep an eye closed, which takes away from the task at hand. With both of them open, you could better focus on things that mattered, such as breathing and aiming. I didn't know if I entirely agreed, but even so, I trusted her judgment better than anyone's, so I'd chosen to do as she told me. No loss in concentration, no difficulties aiming. Whether that was due to keeping my eye open or not didn't really matter.

My job wasn't to actually do any shooting today, but if the situation called for it, I was cleared to take out any security that Clementine ran into and couldn't deal with on her own. For the most part, my job was to be her eyes from a distance, taking lives from afar.

This was our first job off-world, and I'd be damned if I was going to screw it up. Six months working for the organization, and the two of us hadn't let Mulberry down yet. It was bound to happen he'd told us, but so far, our record was clean. Everyone in the guild had been on a botched job at some point or another, but ours had yet to happen. I hoped to keep it that way for as long as possible.

And that included today.

"Thirty-Six, I'm seeing a pair patrolling about twenty meters to your left," I said, training the scope over both of them. As the target reticule touched them, I sent a signal to the HUD of Clementine's goggles, letting her know where they were.

"Roger that, Thirty-Seven," she whispered back, shifting to her right. The property had a lot of wide openings. Clementine hugged the shadows and kept to where there were trees and bushes to hide her. Not the easiest method of entry, or the quietest, but we had to take what we had to work with. In this case, brush and foliage with a dash of security patrols.

Our target was a woman named Primrose Fantigue—by all accounts, one of the wealthiest female entrepreneurs on Epsy.

A closer look over her files showed she was one of the largest drug distributors on the planet, and more importantly, a rival to one of our own clients back on Osiris. That meant that it was only a matter of time before someone sent one an assassin her way. We just happened to land the contract.

According to our reports, another squad had tried to kill

her a few years ago, but they'd botched the job. Still, the attack had left her with an ugly scar across her cheek. She had more than doubled her security afterward, raising the detail from twelve to twenty-five. A wise decision, considering how many people wanted her dead.

This was a career-making job, or career-breaking if things went poorly. Success would solidify our reputations. Failure could mean exposure or death.

This was our biggest job to date. Before now, we'd been given low to mid-tier targets. No one of any significance, but they'd all been dangerous. Mulberry had told us that he'd give us increasingly difficult marks to force us to push past our limits and grow, and it seemed he wasn't lying.

I shifted my view, guiding my scope up the path that Clementine would take. It would pass within five paces of an open-air pool with a small seating terrace. As Clementine approached it, I scanned the area.

"Hold it," I whispered. "Someone is coming out."

Clem froze behind a few bushes, highlighted in a blue silhouette on my scope. Lights shined over the terrace, but they would have a hard time getting any kind of reflection off Clem's charcoal stealth uniform.

One of the glass doors opened, and a man stepped outside. He was in a security outfit, but his tie was loosened, and he had a cigarette in his hand. As soon as he was far enough away from the building, he pulled a lighter out.

"He's alone," Clem whispered softly. "I can take him."

I agreed. I could take him too. The rifle I had picked out allowed for the 600 meters I needed if we could get the target out in the open. It wasn't suppressed, though. Even if it were, the sound would still be loud enough to alert the others. I was only to fire in emergencies.

"Make it quick," I whispered.

She pinged me an affirmative, slipping through the underbrush until she was near the smoking guard. Once she broke cover, she stayed in a crouched position, hiding behind a cabana and a statue of a naked woman as she moved closer, coming up behind him. She was still shorter than I was, and a good head shorter than the guard, but that didn't really matter. She could kill a man twice her size, and he'd never see it coming.

Through the scope, I saw her wrap a gloved hand around the man's mouth, causing him to drop the smoking cigarette while striking the knife into his backside. Two strikes to deflate the lungs and potentially pierce the heart.

They were deep cuts, and he dropped to his knees, instinct taking over as he reached for his wounds instead of a radio or a weapon. He gasped, surprised and desperate, but it was too late.

Clementine held him in place, then ran her knife along his

neck, letting the blood drain out like a butchered animal, holding his mouth until he went limp. When he finally stopped struggling, she dropped the corpse and stood up.

"This is getting too easy," Clem whispered. I couldn't see her face, but I could tell from her voice that she was smirking.

I sighed. "I think you're enjoying this a little too much."

She shrugged. "So? It's good to enjoy what you do for a living. The important thing is to be good at it, and I—" She paused as she tried the glass door that the guard had come through. It opened. "Well, I'm the best at what I do."

I rolled my eyes, leaving the rifle on the ground as I stood. We would come back to pick it up when we were finished. In the meantime, the scope would relay direct video feed to my visor, giving me a continuous bird's eye view of the facility. If the patrols changed or one of them decided to go take a piss, I'd know about it.

"You're clear," Clem said through the comms. "You have about eight minutes to get here before they come back around. You'd better get moving."

"Come on," I said, breaking into a jog. "I can make a hundred and twenty meters in forty seconds."

"It's not a sprint, Thirty-Seven," Clem said, slipping inside the house to get out of sight. "You still need to sneak across the same path that I did."

"Your confidence is heart-warming, Thirty-Six," I said sarcastically, quickly reaching the rope that Clem left for me on the perimeter wall. "Seriously, I'm tearing up over here."

I vaulted the wall, smoothly reached the top, and pulled up the rope. From there, I rolled under the electrically charged fence before dropping to the grass. I kept to a crouch, scrambling for the bushes that flanked a path leading right to the pool terrace where Clem entered the building. I kept to the same route she'd taken.

We had a map of the various motion sensors, but they were mostly in the front of the property. The rear was known to have birds and other animals sneaking in from the wild area outside the walls. After too many false alarms, our target removed them. Bad move on their part.

It did result in heavier security, but thanks to a simple payoff, we had the schedule and turnover times. By paying off two of the guards, they could show up for their shift change, then leave before anyone noticed. That ten-minute window was all we needed to slip in undetected.

I reached the spot where Clem had left the body in less than two minutes and then moved stealthily across the terrace where Clem had opened the door for me.

"Lucky we had a smoker to get the door for us, eh?" she whispered as I slipped inside.

I pulled my goggles up. "Yeah. Lucky. Let's keep our guard

up. We're not finished with this yet."

I pulled my pistol out, chambering a round before nodding at Clem, telling her to lead the way. We moved quietly through the palatial house, going from the gaming room where we had entered into a gallery and then a study.

Most of the place wasn't used during the evenings. Honestly, I would have trouble finding a reason for this much space. I understood needing to have a property where one could host parties and social gatherings, but living here alone? I just couldn't wrap my head around it. Besides, security for a place this big had to be expensive. We'd just demonstrated how it lowered their effectiveness too.

Fantigue's voice carried as we entered her workspace, and it sounded like an angry one-sided conversation. I motioned for Clem to come forward since the target had her back to us. She was leaning over her desk, occasionally bringing her hand down, speaking through her comm.

"I'm not going to calm down, you useless fucking weasel," she said. "That last shipment was short. If the shipments—No, you listen to me. I don't care how you feel about it. This has happened twice! Am I supposed to let you keep fucking me over, Ray? Is that what you want, you piece of shit? I'm starting to think it might be time for me to find another supplier." She paused a few seconds. "I don't give a damn about that! If the next shipment isn't exactly what we ordered, we're going to find somebody else! No, scratch that. If the next shipment doesn't cover what went missing from the last two, you can be sure that I'll hunt you down and take it out of your fucking corpse!" She slammed her comm down, ending the connection.

The very picture of cool-headedness, this woman. I shifted my grip on my weapon as we cautiously approached her.

I had taken the kill last time, so unless the circumstances demanded it, it was Clem's turn.

Fantigue spun around, looking like she was about to storm off, but stopped cold when she saw us. To her credit, she didn't look panicked like most other targets did. She looked angry.

Understandable, I supposed. Her had shipment just come in short, and now there were two people here to kill her.

Not exactly the best day.

"Who the fuck are you?" she asked imperiously, wisely not moving as I had my gun trained on her forehead.

"I'd tell you," Clem said, using the modulator to warble her voice, and sounding a lot like Mulberry. "But I don't actually have a name."

Clem approached, walking directly through my line of sight. Fantigue noticed, probably thinking that it was her chance to act. She jerked towards Clem, trying to grab at her, maybe use her as a shield.

This seemed to happen all the time. Everyone thought we were pushovers because we were small and thin. That was a good thing. It meant they'd never see the next part coming.

Clementine sidestepped the woman's grasp, reaching up and stabbing her knife into Fantigue's arm. The scarred woman staggered, gripping at where the knife dug in deep, letting out a quick yelp.

Clem didn't let up. She grabbed hold of Fantigue's hair and stuck the knife through her lips, cutting her lips on each side to form a kind of permanent smile. From there, she spun the blade around in her mouth, cutting what I guessed was her tongue, and filling her with blood.

The sight of it made me sick.

"No more talking, bitch," said Clementine, almost giggling.

"H-hey!" I said, raising my hand at her. "What are you— what are you doing? Just end it so we can go!"

Clementine sighed, but flicked the knife around into an over-handed grip and stabbed Fantigue in the ribs, near the left kidney. She circled around the woman as she fell to her knees. The final cut went deep into the back. Fantigue's eyes widened at the sudden disbelief of it—that a girl so small could take everything from her.

I felt sick to my stomach, the same way I always did when I watched Clem in action. The wicked smile across her face gave me chills. In these moments, she looked the happiest, as though this was her true home. I clenched my jaw as I looked away, my eyes scanning the area to make sure that none of the security was coming for us. They weren't, and when I glanced back at the two women, Clem was cleaning her knife on one of the unstained parts of the dead woman's shirt.

"Was that really necessary?" I asked when Clem walked towards me.

Clem turned her modulator off and shrugged. "I'm just thorough. Come on. We've got to get out of here."

I nodded, shaking my head as I moved back the way we came. The guards would have returned from their unscheduled break by now, so our way in couldn't be our way out. Even so, I had kept my mind on a handful of different potential escape routes, while memorizing the layout. Back through the wooded area was still our best shot

I motioned for Clem to follow me, and we made our way back to the outside. We came to a halt, hugging the shadows again as a team of four guards jogged past us. They didn't look concerned, but as they passed, one of them was talking into his comm.

"He's not here," one of them said. "Still hasn't reported back."

"Keep looking," one of the men in the middle said. "He

might just be taking another smoke break."

The one in the back grinned. "He's so getting fired for this."

They hadn't found the body yet. They would have the urge to look for a body in a few minutes, and someone would have to report to Fantigue, and then they'd find that body too. We needed to get clear, fast.

We were just a few meters from the wall, and I pointed toward it. Clementine nodded, and as soon as the guards were clear, we ran for it.

I went first, stopping and turning away from the wall, holding my hands out. Clem sprinted for me, jumping into my hands. I heaved upward, letting her get another step on my shoulder.

She mantled the wall and lay prone on top with a leg dangling down for me. I took a few steps back for a running start, sprinted, and reached up to grab her extended leg. She grunted, helping me up, and I finally grasped the top with both hands. Clem slipped over the wall and dropped down on the other side. I landed next to her a second later.

A minute or so after we had cleared the wall, the sound of alarms blared from the property. Men yelled, and dogs barked, but we were already out of reach.

As we made our way through the woods, I didn't say anything. Clem seemed elated, as she always did when we got the job done. For the first time, I didn't feel like pretending that I felt the same.

I had seen what she'd done. I'd seen her do it before, but not like that. Never had I seen her enjoy a kill so much or for so long.

My feelings weren't as secret as I'd meant them to be. When we got back to my rifle, I felt her hand on my shoulder.

"Hey, so what gives?" she asked, pulling her mask away to reveal an annoyed and confused expression.

I shrugged her hand off. "Nothing. It's nothing."

"Come on. We've been around each other long enough for me to know when something's ticking you off." She idly stroked her belt of knives. "What is it? Something I did?"

"Are you kidding me?" I snapped, spinning around to face her and pulling my mask off. "Was it something you did?"

"So, it was. Okay—"

"You stabbed her seven times, and once while she was already on the floor."

"So what? She was the target."

"I don't care. If she were only a target to you, you would have known that she was dead after the first few stabs. Definitely after the sixth."

"I was being—"

"Don't tell me about being thorough." The anger I had been holding in over the past six months bubbled to the surface. My neck throbbed, and my face went red. I could barely stand to look at her, so I just turned around. "You're supposed to be acting like a professional, not playing with your targets. Not pin cushioning them. You always take it too far."

"Hey, what's your problem?" Clementine snapped back. I felt a sudden push at my back, causing me to stumble forward. "You've never complained about how I do my job before."

"I kept hoping you'd slow down, get yourself situated, but you never do. I just—"

She raised her hands. "Look, I do my *job*, and I do it *well*. What the fuck else do you want from me?"

"I want you to be professional!" I barked.

"Fuck being professional," Clem scoffed, pushing at me again, now with both hands. As I looked at her, I noticed a strange, but familiar look in her eyes—the same hunger and passion that burned before she made a kill. The same one that made me sick to see. Something dangerous and ugly, waiting to break out of her.

A bloodlust.

I saw her thumb the dagger on her belt. "Just shut up and leave it alone," she muttered.

"Clem, you need—" I started to say, but I stopped short when she slammed the knife into a fallen log right next to her.

"Don't make me tell you again," she said, her voice devoid of all emotion.

My instincts had my hand gripping my pistol. "Okay," I said, my voice quiet and flat. "Relax."

She stared at me for what felt like too long, but after several seconds, she turned and grabbed the knife, drawing it from the log and placing it back inside her belt. She began walking away, headed towards the shuttle we'd left parked in the clearing near the woods.

I let her put some space between us, and once we were inside the ship, neither of us said a word.

FOURTEEN

I stared at the screen, watching the minutes tick by on the security footage. I'd been playing it at three times the actual speed, but even at that rate, five hours had passed, and I'd barely made a dent in my workload.

Every mission required long hours of preparation, review, and research. At no point had I ever realized just how much of this the job required or just how boring it could be.

I never expected the life of an assassin to be so tedious.

I was on my third coffee and still struggling to stay awake.

It wasn't my fault that things had changed. I never wanted to push Clementine away. I didn't regret it, but it really hadn't been my intention. She had changed over the years, but I always hoped I could get her to change for the better.

She had her demons, but who didn't? None of that was any excuse for what she'd done on our missions together.

Maybe it was therapeutic for her. Maybe she was just a sadist. I honestly couldn't say, because the girl I once knew had become someone else.

I had hoped that standing up to her might wake her up to how she was behaving. Maybe it was vain of me, but I thought I could fix her. I was wrong.

After that mission on Epsy, she had demanded she be given solo work from then on. No more cooperative jobs, and when Mulberry had asked me what I thought about it, I agreed, requesting to work from home.

Clem had been sent off on assignment after assignment, barely spending any time at the complex anymore. Sometimes, she didn't even come back between jobs. Her life had become a cycle of death, and I simply couldn't be a part of it anymore. Not with how she'd chosen to do it. Not with those hungry eyes, so desperate to inflict pain. It was one thing to kill, one thing to take the lives of murderers, rapists, and terrorists, but it was something else to take joy in it.

I paused the footage, taking a note on my pad of a couple of people entering the building, and then resumed the footage.

I had acquired an identity of my own without Clementine—one focused on intelligence gathering and analysis. It had taken months of additional training, and the pay had dropped significantly, but I was fine with all of that. The only reason I'd chosen this life in the first place was that I didn't want to leave her, but with her always away, I saw no reason to continue taking contracts.

Now, my friend—my sister—had made it abundantly clear she did not want me around anymore, and it hurt to know that. And it hurt that I was the cause of that, by snapping at her on Epsy.

Was it my fault?

I paused the video, rubbing my eyes as I leaned back in my seat. I had done what I thought was right at the time, but I hadn't done it for her. It hadn't been out of concern for her, but rather for my own sensibilities. But if I was going to practice my own restraint, maybe being an assassin wasn't the life for me.

Maybe I had been right in pulling away from the killing part of the life and settling for desk work instead. The pay wasn't as good, and I was sitting on my ass most of the time instead of traveling the stars like I'd always wanted.

Had I changed that much? Had my dreams changed, or had a fear of what I'd have to do to realize them made me think I didn't want that anymore?

I looked down at my desk. Mixed in with all the clutter and electronics, my old school pad stuck out. I'd read through the library in it twice over by now, but I still kept it around for reference.

Like many times before, I'd recently picked up *Tales of the Earth: Mankind's Lost Homeworld*. Reading it always put a smile on my face and made me remember my childhood, and I'd often get lost, even now, imagining a planet rich with life, monsters, and magical creatures.

There were all sorts of stories about Earth, besides those in this book, and I'd read most of them. A lot of scholars believed that Earth, or a place upon which this mythical planet was based, could have been the place where humans originally evolved. The only problem was that no one had ever found much proof, one way or the other. There were only vague mentions in ancient writings. Never anything concrete. Still, the thought of such a place exhilarated me, and I found my dreams were often better after a quick read from the book. One day, I wanted to leave this place and search for a planet like the one they talked about in these stories—a place rich with green hills and fields, crystal blue waters, and beautiful skies. There didn't need to be any dragons or flying dogs; just a lovely countryside with kind and welcoming people.

I looked up at the video. I had twelve more hours of footage to check over, but I didn't have to turn in a full report on it for a couple of days.

My ass and legs hurt from not moving out of my seat for most of the afternoon, so I decided to take a break and stretch my muscles. Maybe get a little exercise in while I was at it. I stood up, grabbing my old pad and taking it with me as I made my way to the gym. I switched to exercise clothes, leaving the pad in my locker.

I started with a nice long run. A lot of the others liked to listen to music or maybe watch something while on a treadmill. For myself, I liked the path around the complex, through the neighboring streets and into the garage entrance.

If taken in its entirety, the route might take someone about fifteen minutes to jog the whole way around, but it gave me a sense of tranquility like I was someplace far away.

I took the path around three times, breathing heavily by the end but feeling good. I'd have to start pushing myself harder to make up for the lack of physical training sessions and fieldwork. All this desk time was making me soft.

I made my way back inside. There were a handful of people in the sparring room, but I had no reason to go there, so I avoided it. I headed for the indoor rock-climbing room instead. I wiped the sweat off my hands with a towel and patted them with the chalk. It was weird. When I was alone and didn't have anybody watching or judging me, I found myself working better. I'd even broken Pearl's time on the rock wall, and I'd slowly nudged my way closer to Clementine, who still holds the record.

After I finished my climb, I used my remaining time to practice my stances. I might not be in the field, but it wouldn't hurt to keep my limbs trained and ready.

Finally, I decided to head to the shooting range. Target practice didn't offer much in the way of exercise, but I enjoyed it for the stress relief.

Five rounds went by in a flash. Each one found the target, tagging the head with exact precision, dead center.

Part of me wondered if I should get back into the field again. After five months at the desk, I was beginning to grow sick of these walls, and I had certainly enjoyed traveling between planets. Epsy, Calipso, Mantei, and Shoro, to name a few. The best part of fieldwork was traveling.

I could ask Mulberry for a job. Maybe something off-world, closer to the core system.

Maybe getting out would be good for me.

I leaned into the scope and fired.

Another five rounds, all within the ten-centimeter circle, making a slightly off-center five-pointed star.

I felt good about my aim. It had actually gotten better since I quit going on missions. More practice time, I supposed. But what good were these skills when I couldn't even use them? Maybe I really did need to ask for a job. Maybe it was time.

I winced. The thought of doing missions again just didn't feel as appealing as I wanted it to. Perhaps it was time to find another career. Put the organization behind me and move on to something else. Clementine and I would eventually figure things out, after all. She'd meet me halfway, and then we'd leave together to do something that didn't involve killing people I'd never met before, or at the very least, doing it for a reason besides money.

Was that what had bothered me about the contracts? That it wasn't for any particular purpose? Mulberry had made it a point to only take on criminal cases, but because those jobs always came from the target's rivals or other crime lords, it had created a power vacuum, soon to be filled by the person who hired us. Only very rarely had the job resulted in a drop in crime. Was that what I was missing in my life? Some kind of purpose? A mission to dedicate myself to, like those people in the stories I always read?

Mable had made it out of this life, so why couldn't I?

Well, I still wasn't sure if Mable had been a member of the organization or if her relationship with Mulberry had been something else entirely. The old man refused to talk about any of that.

Even so, there had to be jobs that required the skill-set I'd acquired here. Maybe Mulberry could fix me up with something. I didn't doubt he needed contacts outside of his own people to get information. Maybe I could leave this place and be his eyes somewhere else. At the very least, it might give me the chance to branch out and see the galaxy.

I made my way to the showers and took my time there.

I sighed, letting the warm, steaming water rush through my hair and run over my body, relaxing me. The soothing sound and the calming heat helped my mind go blank, and for a moment at least, I felt at peace. My thoughts drifted to the same place they had so many times before when I needed an escape—sitting with my mother, making cookies. Father had just come home to tell me about his day.

I finished the shower quickly, drying myself off, stopping only to pick up my pad from the locker before heading to the room that Clementine and I had once shared. I plopped down on my bed, taking the pad and activating the V.I.

"Good evening, Miss Abigail," the text read as the still-unsettling smiling face appeared. "How may I help you today?"

"Got any mental gymnastics for me to run through, Angus?" I asked aloud.

"Of course. Here is a selection of mental exercises. Please choose one whichever one you prefer." The text disappeared, and a series of challenges and puzzles appeared in its place.

I ran my eyes over them. I'd completed most of these already, but there were a few I'd continued to put off, saving them for later.

"Abby?" came a voice from the doorway.

I looked up from the pad to see a familiar face staring back at me.

"Pearl!" I exclaimed with a smile, pushing myself up into a sitting position on the bed. "I thought you weren't coming home for a few more days?"

"Back early," she said, cheerily. "Mission successful. Mulberry wanted to see you for dinner tonight. He said he left you a message on your comm but asked me to make sure that you got it. I'd join you, but I really need to sleep. Travel-lag is hitting me pretty hard right now."

"Oh," I said, giving a quick nod. "Okay, thanks, Pearl. I'll be right over."

"I'll see you tomorrow. Let's catch up," she told me, then turned and went towards her room on the far end of the hall.

I took a moment to stretch before checking the message. It relayed the same invitation Pearl had just given me, but it told me dinner would be in his quarters. I knew where it was, having taken messages and delivering equipment, but I'd never been inside.

That part of the complex was strictly off limits to anyone who hadn't been invited, and this was my first invitation. I wondered if this was good or bad. I supposed I would find out soon enough.

I threw on some respectable clothes and made my way through the winding halls to the set of rooms that Mulberry had designated as his own. Once there, I tapped at the door.

A few moments passed, and I was on the verge of knocking again when I heard a hard click. The door opened, and Mulberry stood on the other side. He'd let his stubble grow into something resembling a beard, and he looked tired.

"Make yourself at home," he said, casually.

I smiled politely, not planning on taking him up on that offer. He was barefoot and dressed in comfortable clothes. I felt overdressed in my slacks, dress shirt, and boots.

His quarters certainly intimidated me. I'd read somewhere that to see how a person's mind worked on the outside, one had only to look at their living space because it gave insight into their mind in ways that nothing else could. Mulberry came off stoic and simple, rarely speaking on deeper subjects or the like. Standing in his room, I was beset by droves of artifacts, physical books on philosophy and history, and a brick stone fireplace with a single chair beside it.

The lighting was dim, giving the whole room a rustic, welcoming feel. It felt very much like the man I'd grown to know over the last few years. Rough on the outside, but wise and sincere beneath the surface.

"Can I offer you a drink?" he asked with a welcoming smile. I looked at him, wondering if he was playing some sort of prank or testing me in some way.

If he was, he wasn't giving anything away. He had a wine glass in his hand, and he filled it with sparkling water before I had a chance to respond.

"Yeah, sure," I said.

I was only seventeen, but I'd been drunk a few times and

knew how to handle my alcohol. Mulberry always cautioned against doing anything in excess, but that hadn't stopped Clem and me from stealing a bottle of Red Skeez from Galion's room last year when he was out of the system. We drank the entire thing in a single night and were sick for days afterward.

"How's the desk life treating you?" he asked.

"Honestly?" I asked, taking the glass from him.

He nodded.

"I'm going a bit stir crazy," I said, taking a sip.

Mulberry only laughed. "I can understand that. Your first taste of the life was almost constant action. I can see how going the opposite route might feel tedious and take a bit of getting used to."

I nodded, taking another drink of wine to keep myself from blurting any more of my thoughts. I appreciated Mulberry giving me the job I'd asked for, and I didn't want him to think I was ungrateful.

"Have a seat," he said, gesturing at the chairs beside the table. "Dinner will be here in a minute."

Oh, yeah, dinner, I thought, completely forgetting about it.

Mulberry disappeared behind a door, and I sat down, fidgeting with the armrests as I looked around. What had he called me here for? What did he want from me?

Mulberry returned in a few seconds, carrying two plates.

He placed one in front of me and carried the other to his seat.

He nodded at my plate. "Dig in," he said before taking his own advice.

I glanced down at the plate. The food looked amazing. A thick cut of steak, gleaming in the light like a piece of art. Underneath was an orange mash that smelled of pumpkin, sided with a heap of steamed mushrooms and a pair of asparagus spears wrapped together by strips of Caldaic bacon. Just looking at it made my mouth water.

"Did you make this?" I asked, narrowing my eyes, feeling suspicious again.

He chuckled, taking a moment to swallow what was in his mouth before answering. "I admit I have many talents, but cooking isn't one of them. This is from a local place. I had someone pick it up."

I took a bite of the bacon-wrapped asparagus and closed my eyes.

Mulberry grinned. "Good, isn't it?"

Instead of answering, I attacked the food. I devoured the steak in under a minute, taking a second to wash it down with some water before tearing through the sides like they owed me money. Despite all the many classes I had taken, table etiquette was not one of them—further emphasized as Mulberry calmly cut into his steak when I looked up from my empty plate. I had finished a full minute before he did.

He smiled, finished his food, and cleared our plates, taking a moment to refill my glass before heading back into the kitchen.

I leaned back into my seat, full of the best meal I'd eaten in forever.

Mulberry returned with a pair of plates. The one that he put in front of me had a brownie with a scoop of ice cream on top, and I was hungry all over again.

"How was the steak?" he asked before I could dig in.

I raised my eyes up from the brownie with the ice cream slowly melting on top of it. "Oh, it was fantastic. Best food I've had in a while."

Considering the life I'd lived, it wasn't saying much, but it was enough to drag a smile to Mulberry's face.

I cleared the brownie from my plate slower than I had the rest, but I was still faster than Mulberry. I imitated him as he cleaned his mouth with his napkin, placing it on the empty plate, and sipping from his glass. I looked down. I'd been pushing a thought down all evening, but as the night was coming to a close, I just couldn't keep it bottled anymore.

"So," I started, clearing my throat softly. "Do you know when Clementine is coming back?"

There was a pause, and I knew that whatever Mulberry had to say probably wouldn't make me very happy. The look in his eyes told me that much, at least.

He sighed and took another, rather long, sip from his wine like he was trying to gather his thoughts. "I got a message from her after she completed her last assignment. Apparently, she's decided not to return. As she put it, she's found a new venture that better suits her lifestyle." He cleared his throat and scratched at his jaw. "She won't be coming back."

My face went slack as my hands settled down on the armrests of the chair. I took a deep breath, not knowing what to say.

"I know this isn't easy for you to hear," he said, quietly.

"This is—" I paused. "This is why you asked me here tonight, isn't it?"

He nodded.

The move had probably been inevitable. Clem's ambition had always been to leave this place. I'd just thought she would take me with her. How could she abandon me here? I thought she'd only needed some time to herself, but this—this was permanent. This was forever. How could she leave me behind so easily?

Wasn't she still my sister?

I felt a sudden pain in my chest.

"Uh," was the only sound to come from my mouth as I looked down, fighting back a growing lump in my throat. I cleared it before my emotions could bubble up to the surface. I wasn't about to embarrass myself in front of Mulberry. "I guess—" I paused, trying to stay collected. "—it's for the best, right? I-if that's what she wants."

Mulberry nodded, his eyes drifting to his plate. He twirled his glass in his hands but didn't take a drink. "It came as a surprise to us, but we agreed to let her go. Your sister is an independent young woman, and she's always done things differently."

That was putting it lightly.

"She's capable, and I'm sure that she'll succeed in any venture she chooses," he said.

They were empty words, and we both felt it. I knew that Mulberry saw right through me, and he was just trying to soften the blow. "You don't have to lie about who she is," I said, narrowing my eyes on the table.

We were quiet for a while, sitting together with bowls of melted ice cream. I was so angry, and it rose in me like a fire, burning in my chest.

But then, to my surprise, Mulberry reached out around the table and placed a hand on my wrist, and suddenly the heat in me began to fade. My eyes slowly lifted to meet his, and he gave me a simple nod of understanding. The same eyes that had seen through me when I was an orphaned child, saw through me now, and they broke me.

Hot, angry tears slipped down my cheeks, and there was nothing I could do to stop them.

"Clem has her own path to follow," he said, even as I struggled to keep my composure. "It won't be an easy one, but she has made her decision, and we must accept it. You have your own path, Abigail."

I reached up to wipe my cheeks and felt a sob escape my throat.

I heard his chair scrape across the floor, and another surprise struck me as his arms wrapped around my shoulders. I reached out and held him, as more sobs wracked my chest.

"It's my fault she's gone," I whispered into his shoulder.

He placed his hand on my back. "It's not. I promise you, it's not."

I nodded, sucking in a shaky breath and clearing the tears from my cheeks with the backs of my hands.

Part of me hated Clem, but the other half loved her, and that piece of me would mourn today for quite some time.

I wanted to ask why things had to be this way, why she had to be so broken and wrong, but I didn't. I just kept crying into Mulberry's shirt. The old man had always been there for me. He was the father I'd always wanted, and Pearl, a mother figure. We were the strangest sort of family, but I knew in my heart, there was love here. I knew because tonight there had been good food and ice cream, and a tender man who cared enough to hug me and tell me that it wasn't my fault.

Mulberry smiled at me, picking up my unused napkin and using it to wipe the rest of the tears from my cheeks. "You get some sleep now, kiddo. It's getting late."

FIFTEEN

I rubbed my eyes. I'd been staring at this screen for hours now, and there was no end in sight. Sometimes, working as a researcher meant days and days of tedious, boring tasks. The job would get done eventually, and then I could relax.

I glanced over the screen, holding a real-time satellite visual of the city of Ruto. It was night, and I woke up early to get some exercise in before finishing off a report for this particular operation.

It wasn't like I had anything better to do with my time, but even so, I'd been working this case for a solid month. I wished I could take some time away from it.

Apparently not. Law enforcement vehicles were easy to spot and track. The unmarked ones were a different story. They looked like your average vehicles, only with a few key differences. Spotting them took an accurate eye, but I was pretty good about it. The way they drove, their brand of tires. I could usually spot them if I paid attention.

An alert came in, pulling my attention from the screen. I

flipped the visual over to see the call then groaned.

Numbers Thirty-Eight and Thirty-Nine, otherwise known as Alonso and Bart, the lowest ranking idiots in the guild.

I reluctantly accepted the call.

"Are we clear?" a man's voice asked over the encrypted comm. "Control? Are you there? We need an escape route! We have security after us!"

"Hold position, Thirty-Eight and Thirty-Nine," I said, clearly irritated. "Pulling up mission data and establishing escape route."

"Hurry!" said Number Thirty-Nine.

"I don't see any of them," Thirty-Eight said. "I think we can go."

"I said, hold position," I insisted. "Don't make me tell you again."

"There's nobody here," he said.

I scanned the data from the surveillance program in seconds, surprised by the sheer incompetence before me. "Gods. This is bad. You botched this entire job."

"It wasn't our fault!" insisted Number Thirty-Eight. "Will you just get us out of here? That's your job!"

Bart's voice grated me, and I wanted to turn the system off. Instead, I lost my patience. "I'm not the one who tripped every single alarm within a two-kilometer radius by setting off that explosion, am I?" I asked, rather curtly.

No answer.

"You two got yourselves into this mess, so if you just follow my instructions, I can get you out of it, but I swear to the gods if you argue with me again, I'll let you clean it up yourselves. Understand?"

Still no response.

"Well?" I asked.

"Understood," said Number Thirty-Eight.

I counted the time down, and after fifteen seconds, I keyed the comm again. "Okay, you can move out, but keep your speed at a cool eighty kilometers per hour. Any faster, and you'll get tagged by the speed cams, and you'll have cops all over you in a matter of seconds."

"Copy that, Station. Moving out now."

The car slid into traffic.

I shook my head. These idiots had no clue what they were doing. "Keep to the north route. I sent an anonymous tip about your vehicle speeding on East Forty-Fifth. That should keep the authorities running over that one stretch of road for a while, so keep your current speed, and don't attract any attention, and you should be in the clear. Do you understand?"

The comm keyed on their side. "Yes, Sation," Thirty-Nine said. "We're trusting you."

You probably wouldn't if you knew who I was, I thought. It was the middle of the night, so the roads were deserted except for downtown. That was where the clubs were, so it was entirely normal to see droves of vehicles and people coming and going at all hours, but the same couldn't be said of this part of the city. That's why it had struck me as odd when I saw three vehicles careening out of a small side road at two in the morning, each of them identical makes and models.

"Thirty-Eight and Thirty-Nine, did you kill all the alarms before going into the target's house?" I asked.

"Yes, of course," Thirty-Eight said.

"Even the silent alarm that rings the target's security company instead of the police?"

"The what?" Thirty-Nine asked.

I rolled my eyes, checking through the dossier for this particular mission.

The building's alarms were mostly wired to call the police in the event of a break-in. Inside the bedroom, though, there was a silent alarm that called the target's security company instead. A security company that consisted mainly of former Union military, with a high average of dishonorable discharges.

It was the kind of security that shot first and asked questions later. Not something you wanted to deal with on a stealth mission.

"Never mind," I said, picking up a set of vehicles in pursuit. "Just a heads-up. It looks like you have three hostile vehicles coming at you from the north, currently about ten clicks from your location but closing fast. They didn't show up on my radar until you broke cover, so it's safe to assume they have some sort of visual on the whole situation as well. I'll keep you updated."

"Roger that, Station. We'll keep our eyes open."

I scanned across the area, making sure once more that none of the authorities were patrolling the area. It was both good and bad news that they weren't. Good news for the two men whose lives I was watching over like the universe's most under-qualified guardian angel. Bad news since it allowed these newcomers to do as they pleased without having to worry about the cops.

I zoomed back to the three incoming cars, now only five clicks away. They stopped, forming a sort of blockade across the road. I sighed, finally finding Thirty-Eight and Thirty -Nine a road that would lead them around it.

"Heads up. I've just highlighted a road on your map that should get your around the blockade ahead," I told them. "Once you turn off North, there aren't any speed cams, so you have to punch it to beat a police vehicle coming around in that direction. You'll have to time it."

"Understood, Station," Thirty-Eight said.

They reached the intersection and turned off, immediately picking up speed. Watching the police car, they had about thirty seconds to get back to North before they were seen.

It took about ten seconds for the thugs at the blockade to realize they were being circled around by their quarry. They scrambled to get back into their vehicles and resume the chase. Thankfully, this put the enemy behind them instead of ahead. It would make the rest of this a little easier.

I noted a small problem with my plan. While the two idiots still had to maintain the speed limit to avoid being noticed by the cams, the security team didn't.

"Be advised, Thirty-Eight and Thirty-Nine, you now have pursuers en route. Maintain your current speed but turn left at the next exit and speed up from there. Understand?"

"Roger that, Station."

Moments later, the pursuing vehicles divided into two lanes behind them and opened fire.

I softly cursed.

"Station, we're taking fire here!" exclaimed Bart.

"Still your fault," I grumbled into the comm. "Take the next right. I've already dispatched the drones. They should be there soon."

"We'll try to hang on," said one of them.

I checked the location of the three armed drones currently

flying across the city. They wouldn't be enough to take down the vehicles on their own, but they'd serve as a distraction long enough to give them the slip.

I breathed in deeply as Thirty-Eight and Thirty-Nine's vehicle came into view. They were moving dangerously fast. Even from a thousand meters in the air, I could see the sparks from the gunfire hit their doors.

I followed the road behind them with my drone's scope until I found the leader of the three cars.

"We need some cover now, Station! What's the fucking hold up?" asked Thirty-Nine.

I chose to ignore them, focusing instead on the drones. They were arriving now, speeding to meet the oncoming vehicles.

I took aim at the frontmost cab, tagging it with the aiming program, followed by the other two. This would send precise targeting information to the drones. All I had to do was give the command to pursue.

I keyed it in, and the drones began their descent.

It only took them a few seconds to reach the vehicles, and when they did, the little bots used their onboard flamethrowers to send a wave of fire at the vehicle.

A second later, the first car swerved, cut right, and then flipped, rolling over and over again, so much that I thought it might not end.

The second car didn't have time to stop. It swerved right and left the road, surviving a few seconds before it hit a bump and spun around, crushing its side into a light fixture.

The third vehicle had time to dodge both its disabled comrades and continue the pursuit of Thirty-Eight and Thirty-Nine.

Not for long.

All three drones convened on the last remaining vehicle, immediately unloading what remained of their incendiary liquid in a single, bloody burst. The fire covered the glass, blocking the driver's view, and while I couldn't see much from all the light and smoke, the result was about to become very clear.

The vehicle slammed into the wall of a nearby bar, exploding dust and debris into the air and sending people screaming into the street.

In seconds, my team veered off into another road, escaping the busy intersection. On my orders, they quickly filed into an alleyway. "Thirty-Eight and Thirty-Nine, proceed to the evac point. You know the drill."

"Thanks, Station! That was some amazing work with the drones."

I cringed at the compliment but didn't respond. In case of situations like this, we tried to have multiple exit strategies in place. They weren't always available, especially off-world, but this job had taken place in our city, so we had everything from drones to additional pick-up locations. Once they were out of their vehicle, I'd kill the cab remotely, and the two of them would hike it to another transport. A different make, and a different model.

I turned my attention back to the other cars. No sign of movement from the first, but the second had its door open, and I could see someone on the grass, lying on their stomach.

"Sorry," I whispered. I didn't know these people, and honestly, I had no idea whether they deserved any of this, but they'd been protecting a very dangerous man, and that had put them here on my screen.

I touched my comm, changing the channel. "Number One, are you there?"

"I am, Twenty-Nine, what's the status?" Mulberry asked, his gruff voice sounding ragged.

Over the last year, my ranking in the organization had grown, but that was true of almost everyone. Mulberry believed competition bred success, although I didn't find myself wanting to outperform anyone. I just did what I was told and tried my best. The added rank had happened on its own.

"Complications have been dealt with," I said. "Operatives are clear and coming home."

Mulberry sighed. "I want you and the two operatives reporting to me first thing in the morning."

"Understood," I answered.

I ended the connection and looked back into the scope. Thirty-Eight and Thirty-Nine were already on the move, leaving the alley and heading away.

Given tonight's bungle, I wondered what Mulberry would say to them tomorrow.

Whatever it was, I just hoped I didn't get wrapped up in their stupidity.

* * *

Mulberry hadn't been kidding about wanting to see us first thing in the morning. I'd barely gotten four hours of sleep before my comm crackled with the old man calling me to his office. Alonso and Bart were already there, fidgeting in the seats in front of the oak desk.

Tension hung thick in the air. Mulberry looked calm, but I sensed an undercurrent of anger in him, simmering just below the surface. I sat as far in the corner as I could manage, trying to stay away from the impending storm.

"Now that we're all here, let's get started," he said. "Alonso, tell me what happened at the target's apartment."

I looked away. The sight of the two of them still made me sick.

Alonso sat up straight in his chair. "The schematics said that the best point of entry was through the back, boss. The building didn't have a service elevator, but it did have a service staircase that doubled as an emergency exit. We took that and—"

"He wasn't even home!" Bart blurted out. "The intel was all wrong!"

They both looked at me like it was my fault.

I narrowed my eyes. "Excuse me?"

"Well, ain't it true?" asked Alonso. "The file you gave us says the target was supposed to be home inside his study. We checked everywhere."

"I see," I said, trying to keep my calm. "And exactly what time did you arrive?"

They both looked at each other. "Fifteen after seven," said Bart.

I let out a sigh as my eyes turned to Mulberry. The old man shook his head at the two boys.

Their eyes widened. "But the report said he'd be home!" exclaimed Alonso.

"No," I answered. "It said eight. He'd be home after eight. He went out tonight with a woman to a show, but we expected him home between eight and nine."

The two of them were dumbstruck, probably lost as to how they could so royally screw everything up.

I checked my pad. "But that's not the worst of it," I continued. "The alarm wasn't even triggered by his security team or anyone else in the vicinity. It was automatic."

"What?" asked Alonso.

I blinked at him, looking bored. "You forgot to disable the system. It was a built-in alarm in his study. You tripped it when you went inside. I typed all of this in your file, including how to disable it."

Mulberry nodded, leaning farther back in his seat as he turned his attention back to Alonso. "Gods alive," he said, crossing his arms. "You two idiots really butchered this job. Talk about a fucking pair. You're both suspended for the next month. Docked pay. I'd strip more of your rank if you weren't already at the bottom of the list, but since I can't, I'll just have to find something else to motivate you."

"B-but, sir!" Alonso begged.

"Out!" snapped Mulberry, snapping his fingers and pointing towards the door.

The pair got to their feet and quickly ran to the exit like they were escaping. "As for you," said Mulberry, turning his eyes on me. He paused, letting a slight smirk slide across his cheek. "Nice work."

I smiled in return and gave a simple nod. "Just doing my job."

"And a fine job it is," he replied.

I got to my feet, feeling fairly good about myself and made

my way into the hall.

As I neared the corner, heading to my room, I heard a voice call out from behind me.

"Hey, wait up!" Alonso shouted.

My stomach dropped at the sound of his voice and the heavy footfalls of him jogging to catch up with me. I stopped and briefly closed my eyes, trying to compose myself.

"Abigail, hey," he said, walking up to me. "I wanna word about what you said in there."

I raised an eyebrow. "Just a word?"

He shrugged. "We're all on the same team here, but you threw us to the dogs. What's your problem? What did I do to you?"

"I have a lot of work to do," I said, not wanting to get into all of this right now. "So, maybe another time."

I turned around, moving to make my exit.

"You don't have to be such a bitch about it. It's not like you could do what we do. I heard about how you choked in the field, so they put you on the desk. Makes sense you'd be jealous, I guess. Hey, are you listening to me?"

I was already walking, knowing that if I stayed a second longer, I might do something I'd regret.

"I'm talking to you, you little idiot!" Alonso barked, and suddenly I felt a firm hand on my shoulder.

He really shouldn't have done that.

I spun around, immediately bunching my shoulders and bringing my fists up. I let him fall forward, towards me and launched my knee into his belly.

He wheezed, gasping for the precious air I'd stolen from him. "You fucking bit—"

I cut him off, stepping in close and grabbing his shoulders with both hands, quickly raising him with my side and slamming him to the floor with a firm hip toss.

"I see why you're Number Thirty-Eight," I muttered, drawing my sidearm and flicking the safety off with my thumb.

I didn't always carry my weapon around the complex with me, but I'd been planning to head to the range after the meeting.

Lucky me.

Bart came running from down the hall, but he stopped when he saw his friend on the floor and my barrel aimed at his face. Bart's eyes widened at the sight of me.

"Back up," I ordered, and Bart immediately complied, raising his hands and moving away.

"Hey! Okay! Geez!" he stuttered.

"I said *back up!*" I snapped, and he jumped a few steps away from me. I kept my gun on him until he was several meters into the hall, giving me enough space to get closer to Alonso.

I leaned in and pressed my barrel into his shoulder—the

same shoulder that Clem had dug a knife into years ago. "Come near me again, and I'll kill you both," I said, almost in a whisper. "No one will care. Better yet, no one will know. You're both already on everyone's shit-list. Remember that."

He groaned in response.

I shot a quick look at Bart as he took a step back.

"Oh," I said just before leaving. "And not that it matters, but I volunteered for the desk."

I kept my composure for as long as it took for me to go around a corner. After that, I started moving faster, practically running for my room. *Our* room. The only place I felt truly at peace in the whole world.

Once I reached it, I stepped in and closed the door behind me. I pressed my back into it, sinking down with the gun still in my hand and closed my eyes.

I wasn't crying, but that sick, nauseated feeling didn't lift. I didn't think it would for a while. It wasn't for them. They were assholes who were too used to having their own way.

This was something else, and it didn't take me long to realize that what I had just done—well, it felt good.

A thrill and excitement pulsed through me. Had I missed using this weapon so much that the mere taste sent endorphins through my brain?

Or was it something more, perhaps? Vindication?

Retribution?

Justice?

I sighed, leaning back against the door, tapping my head lightly against the hard surface.

"I need a fucking shower," I whispered to myself.

Sixteen

A week had passed since the meeting with Mulberry, Alonso, and Bart, and I found myself back in the field on another case. Mulberry granted my request to leave the compound and the desk, giving me the ability to go outside and perform a little reconnaissance.

There were reports this target spent a few nights a week at a mistress's residence off-site, so I made a note to find where the woman lived to see if there wasn't a better shot at him there.

The more I thought about it, the more I realized that maybe research and intelligence was my true calling. I liked studying. I liked finding out about the targets. Reading up on the various worlds across Union space wasn't as good as actually visiting them, but I didn't have to kill anyone with my own hands, and I also didn't have to sit behind a desk and stare at a screen.

Instead, I was back in the field, armed with a pad and a camera instead of a rifle, although I still brought one with me for emergencies. This was a challenging job, but I decided I liked it as soon as I started, and I never wanted to go back.

I looked over the complex, seeking out the motion detectors and cameras.

My job right now was to chart a safe path for anyone who needed to infiltrate the area.

Were the patrols infrequent? How many cameras? Did the alarms connect to the city grid? If so, we could hack them. If not, we'd have to get around them. No matter the problem, our people had the resources and knowledge to always get the job done. I made another note about the fence and then moved on.

The security for this building wasn't available to the public, so it was my job to gather whatever I could and report back.

I found the woman's address. It was a proper house, which immediately made it a better option. I started looking over the home's infrastructure. Nothing serious regarding security. It had a simple intruder alarm that alerted the local authorities with a call box located outside the house.

Simple enough to disable.

I leaned back with a scowl. The analyst working this mission should have identified the house as the best option instead of making me run straight for the target's work building. It would have saved us all some time.

I keyed in the information and sent it back to the analyst. They'd relay the data to the field agent, and that would be the end of it. My job was done.

I got to my feet and took off for the transit terminal. It would take me a few hours to get home, which is why I'd brought my pad with me. Plenty of time to read. This was the best the part.

* * *

"Miss Abigail?" came a voice from the other side of my door.

I opened it just waking up, and scratched the side of my jaw. Standing there nervously was a smallish boy that looked like he was about fifteen years old, with red hair and freckles. Since I didn't recognize him, I had to assume he was a trainee and fresh off the street.

"How can I help you?" I asked.

"Miss Pearl said Mr. Pryar needs to speak with you. He's on your personal line," said the boy.

I nodded. "Thanks."

He ran off as I walked to the side table and retrieved my comm from the drawer, placing it in my ear while taking a moment to stretch. I connected to the secure channel.

"Abigail, is that you?" asked Mulberry.

I could already tell something was wrong. His voice and tone were off, almost scratchy.

"Yes, it is. What seems to be the problem?" I instinctively pressed at my earpiece to hear more clearly.

I'd seen Mulberry in a lot of moods. Angry, emotionless,

even happy on a few occasions. But I'd never heard him sound jumpy, and it made me nervous.

"Are you alone?" he asked.

I saw the door was still open, so I quickly shut it and walked all the way back to my bed. "I am now. What's going on?"

"It's Mable," he said, flatly.

I paused at the sound of her name. "*Sister* Mable?"

I wasn't sure what else to say. It had been years since I saw her last, but not a day went by that I didn't wonder how she was doing.

"That's the one," he said. "She's still at the orphanage, far as I'm aware. I need you to find her and bring her to the complex as fast as you can."

I frowned. "What's going on, Mulberry? Is she in danger?"

He sighed. "I just had a conversation with one of my old contacts. There's—" His voice dropped for a second, and I wondered if I'd lost him, but he simply cleared his throat. "There's a contract out on her."

My eyes widened. "W-what?"

"She wasn't always part of the Church, Abby. She used to work with me, even before I started this place when we were young and stupid. We both slipped up, but she went straight, changed her name, tried to live a better life. That's the real story to it, but someone's found out about her."

I tried to process what I was hearing, but it was too much, too fast. Images of the woman I knew raced through my mind, each of them clashing with the revelation before me—she had been an assassin like me and Mulberry. How could someone so gentle, ever be a part of this life?

"Look," he said, his voice calming a little. "I'm off-planet. I can't get home until tomorrow at the latest, and this hit is supposed to happen sometime over the next three days. I need you to find Mable and bring her back right away. Can you do that?"

I paused for a second. "Isn't she prepared for this sort of thing? She must have a way out of there."

"I have reason to believe her safehouse is exposed. I'm sure she could handle herself in the Church, but there will be a team waiting for her when she arrives at the dead drop. We need to get to her before she leaves the church, or we risk letting her walk right into an ambush."

I nodded, even though he couldn't see. "I follow, sir," I assured him, already grabbing my shoes.

"Call me when it's done," he said, sounding relieved. "Take the fastest shuttle we have." There was a short pause. "And don't call the orphanage, whatever you do. The lines are likely being monitored and will only cause us problems. No matter what, we can't compromise our ability to protect her. That means—"

"I can't let anyone see who I am," I finished.

"If they do, you can't let them walk away," he replied.

"Yes, sir."

"I'll authorize whatever expenses you make. Don't tell anyone where you're going or why. If they ask, have them call me directly. I'll have my comm with me at all times. Get this shit done, Abby, and do it fast."

"I understand," I said, heading for the door.

I broke into a jog on my way to the armory. I picked up a pistol with a suppressor, a few smoke grenades, and my old combat suit. It had been a while since I'd used the uniform, but if there was a team coming for Sister Mable, I wasn't going to take any chances.

On the way to the shuttle bay, I made a requisition to release one for my use. After a quick authorization from Mulberry, I stepped into the craft and primed the engines. I glanced down at my hip to see the smoke grenade, wondering if I should have brought it but shrugged and decided it couldn't hurt.

While the turbines spun up, I slipped on my suit and a fresh set of clothes to conceal the armor. Everything was a little more snug than usual, but I didn't mind it. For whatever reason, the suit felt natural like I'd somehow missed it.

As the ship lifted off the ground and launched into the air, nervousness washed over my chest, flushing my cheeks. This was the first time I was returning to the orphanage, and the first time

I would see Sister Mable—and for some reason, I found that aspect of the mission more frightening than the rest.

* * *

Arriving near the old gate surrounding the orphanage and its many buildings, I was beset by an unexpected sense of nostalgia.

I couldn't remember when I first arrived here as a child. I'd only been about five years old, but all of my best and worst memories were of this place, and for the most part, the good outweighed the bad. Waiting in line for breakfast. Marching up to the schoolroom with the other kids. Asking annoying questions to Sister Amber and hearing her sigh in frustration as the other kids giggled.

I had fond memories of coming outside to play with Clementine. Hearing her talk about what she'd learned from the sisters who seemed to speak around us without thinking. I'd rarely understood any of it, but Clem had always had a sharper mind for things like that.

I smiled, circling around the massive cathedral before setting the shuttle down at one of the two landing docks down the street. In that time, a quick scan revealed no sniper's nests or high cover targets to worry about. Only ground personnel, which I could mostly avoid if I played things the right way.

From the dock, I jogged to the rear entrance behind the

church complex. It took longer than I cared for, but it was the safest way to get inside.

As the church came into view, I recalled one instance where I'd tried to scale the bell tower as a girl. I was clumsy back then, and I'd gotten stuck on a window about halfway up. It was the most afraid I'd ever felt in my whole, short life. If Clem hadn't helped me, I wasn't sure what I would have done.

"If only seven-year-old me could see me now," I whispered, stepping through the rear gate.

Clem apologized to me later that evening for daring me to do it. I told her that I'd been the one stupid enough to accept the challenge, so I deserved the grounding that the sisters gave me when they eventually got me back down.

A bittersweet memory, that one. It was the first time I'd felt like Clem and I were sisters instead of just friends. We became almost inseparable after that.

I spotted a large, military grade van along the side street to the orphanage. That made more sense than a shuttle, considering how landing one so close to the building would only draw attention from the police.

The team—whoever they were—had already arrived. I was late to the party.

There was a decent chance that if anyone was inside that thing, they'd already spotted my arrival. I'd lost the element of surprise.

Still, they might not know why I was here or whether I was even a threat. I wasn't exactly imposing.

I made sure that my holster remained hidden underneath my jacket.

I stepped out of the shuttle, holding my pad and looking down at it like my whole life was crammed into this tiny piece of technology. For all anyone knew, I had a set of adoption papers on this thing and simply couldn't take my eyes off of them. I completely ignored the armored vehicle as I made for the entrance.

When I was halfway there, a man in a security uniform spotted me and approached. I didn't recognize the logo, but I already knew it was fake.

"Excuse me, miss?" he asked with guarded concern in his voice. "What are you doing here?"

"Hm?" I looked up like I didn't know exactly where the voice was coming from. "Are you talking to me?"

The man stood a few meters from his vehicle, a fake smile on his face as he approached.

There was a bulge in his jacket and belt, indicating a weapon. "Yes," he said, still walking to me from across the yard. "You shouldn't be here right now. This area is off limits. I'll have to ask you to leave."

I tried to look surprised. "Oh, I see," I said, touching my chest and widening my eyes.

"I'll walk you back to your vehicle," he said, slyly, and he motioned to where I had parked my shuttle.

My hand stayed close to my open jacket. "I can't believe this. I came here to ask about adopting. I'm in the market, you know. Well, my husband and I. We're newlyweds."

"That's nice," he said.

I began to turn away from him, but only enough to slip my hand between my jacket and grab my pistol. With the other, I took out my pad. "Oh, let me show you the little girl I was looking at," I said, bringing the pad high into the air. His eyes followed it away from me, and I took out the gun and shot him through the head.

He dropped to the grass, face-forward.

I squatted down next to him. His weapon had been silenced, but it was a military-issued .45. He had police-issued body armor, but it still had nothing on my own equipment. Whoever he and his friends were, they probably hadn't expected to run into someone like me.

I pulled his comm from his ear and put it in mine. Someone else was already talking.

"—finished with that witness yet? Barry? Hey, man, you there?"

A short pause.

"Fuck. Okay, I'm coming outside. You'd better be dead or so help me gods," said the voice.

I hurried to the rear entrance, holding my pistol up and at the ready as I slipped through the door this man had been watching.

His people would come to check on him soon, which meant I'd have to be fast before things really got out of hand.

If these men had only just arrived, there was a decent chance they'd caught everyone during dinner. That was good because it meant I could reasonably predict where most of the kids would be unless they'd been moved.

Mable generally had her dinner in her office, although I was pretty certain I wouldn't find her there.

Still, I decided to check there first, just in case, since it was nearby.

I hurried up a short flight of carpeted stairs, weapon ready and my eyes darting to every available entrance. I knew this place like the back of my hand, so it made things all the more easier. I had the advantage, however slight.

A quick glance in Mable's office was enough to know she wasn't there, but I did spot a plate of uneaten food on the desk.

"I found Barry!" sprang a voice in my ear. "Looks like a clean shot. Professional hit."

"Find the nun and sweep the floor!" barked another.

The nun? Did they mean Mable? Had they still not found her?

"One of the nuns told me where her room is. I'm on my way there!"

Mable's room was two floors down. I made my way down quickly, my boots moving over the steps without a sound.

I was about to reach her quarters when the door creaked open, and I huddled with my back to the nearest wall, next to the door.

Since these people had already cleared this area, the guard wouldn't think to do it again. I just had to wait here long enough to—

I retrieved a small stun baton from my side, waiting for him to step inside the room, aiming at the back of his head.

A quick tap of the trigger sent a shock through his entire body, causing him to double over. I drew a garrote from my jacket sleeve and wrapped it around his neck, leaping onto his back with my full body weight to strangle him. He tried to reach me but couldn't, and instead stumbled into the nearby walls. I couldn't see his face, nor did I want to, but I imagined the fear in his eyes as he realized he might not survive this moment.

He dropped to his knees, and I gripped the chord with all the force I could give until finally he closed his eyes and fell against the carpet.

I shoved him out of the way, heavy as he was, and pulled the handle down enough to crack the door. Then, using my foot with my back against the adjacent wall, I pushed the door all the way open, staying out of sight.

Nothing.

The room was empty, but another door was open on the other side. I knew that one led to a branching hallway and then on to the main office.

I heard someone clear their throat on the other side. A gruff, deep voice saying something inaudible to himself.

At that moment, the comm in my ear sputtered alive with talk. "Spotted her in the head office! She's running! I'm on it!"

I cursed. Normally, I'd try to lure the nearby guard into this room, but there wasn't enough time. I'd have to get through him and make it to Mable before it was too late.

Easing the door open, I spied the armed soldier holding his rifle by the strap around his neck as his hands rested on the barrel. Good. He wasn't on guard or ready which meant it would take him time to react.

Time enough to get in close.

I checked my stun baton, but it still wasn't finished charging. That meant I'd have to use the knife if I wanted to keep things quiet.

Hesitantly, I withdrew my blade. I'd have to be like

Clementine. I wasn't strong enough to strangle him without the baton, after all.

I took a quick, steady breath and exhaled.

Immediately, I bolted from the door and into the hall, moving quickly and staying low, my steps quiet and soft.

The man began to turn when I was halfway to him. By the time his eyes were on me, I'd slid beside him along the smooth wooden floor, and before he could react, I sent the dagger into his crotch where the leg met the pelvis. The armor was thin there, and the blade eased into him without much resistance.

There was also a major artery, making the following moment significantly messier.

He yelped in surprise, dropping partially to the floor, and I leaped from my feet and took him by the arm, raising it high enough to stab him twice in the armpit. From there, he gasped while going for his own knife, but I stuck mine through his hand and stabbed the floor, securing him there.

He attempted to scream, but I already had the cord around his throat, choking him. A moment later, he was on the floor, the same as the last one.

I got up and glanced at his face. He looked innocent, almost like a child. Almost peaceful.

I pulled the dagger free of him, then reached higher to his neck and stabbed with my full force, piercing his throat and spilling what remained of his life.

Before he had a chance to hit the floor, I started moving.

I approached the other end of the hall. As I neared the doorway, I slowed my pace and checked my breathing, trying to stay as quiet as possible.

The door was already open.

There were no sounds from inside. Had they already moved on?

I peeked around the corner. Twice the size of Mable's room, its walls were lined with decorative statues. I always wondered what the point of those were. They only sat there, useless, doing nothing. It took me a moment to realize that most of them were prayer shrines, each representing a different god, and each given an offering. It had been so long since I'd been here that I'd already forgotten about them. Now that I tried to remember, it truly seemed like a lifetime ago.

As I took in more of the room, one of the men was lying face-down on the floor but barely seemed to be moving.

I checked my blind spots before going in but couldn't see anyone else. I kept my weapon trained on the squirming soldier as I moved closer to him. Maybe he had information I could—

A small barrel pressed into the back of my head, and I froze.

"Drop the gun," a woman said, and my eyes narrowed. I

knew that voice.

I dropped my pistol to the floor before slowly turning around. A familiar set of eyes met mine.

"Sister Mable?" I asked.

"Abigail?" she answered, lowering the gun a few centimeters while still keeping it raised on me. "What are you doing here? Speak quickly."

She still looked exactly the same, although I was certain I'd grown enough to warrant a pause. She was still beautiful and determined, the same as when I knew her.

I lowered my hands. "Mulberry heard someone was after you, so he sent me to bring you home with us. He said they've got eyes on your safehouse."

She hesitated, and I could see the distrust in her eyes. All those years working in the shadows had made her naturally skeptical, and I understood that.

"Mable," I said, slowly raising my hands. "It's me. Really. I'm not here with these men. I'm here for you. To get you out. I swear it."

She swallowed, twisting her lips as she studied me. "Okay, Abigail," she finally said, allowing herself to relax a little. "You'll have to forgive me, dear. It's instinct at this point."

I smiled and offered her a hug. She came forward and wrapped her arms around my shoulders. "I'm glad you're safe,

Sister Mable," I told her.

"That makes two of us," she said, and I could tell she was smiling. As she pulled away, her eyes were suddenly glassy. "Look at you," she whispered, stroking my cheek and running her fingers through my hair. "Already so grown up. Feels like yesterday when I left you."

I bit my bottom lip and forced a smile. "I should have visited, but—"

She shook her head. "You and I both, but let's focus for now and catch up later."

"Right," I agreed. "We need to get you out of here."

"Help me with that one," she said, pointing to the unconscious guard.

"Sure," I said, grabbing the legs while she took the arms. He was heavier than both of us combined, but Mable had some strength in her legs that I didn't expect.

We brought the guard into the side closet, then shut the door behind him. "I know Sister Murphy has the key to this somewhere around here," she muttered, quickly searching through the desk drawers. "Aha!" she exclaimed, lifting the key to show me.

I answered with a smile.

She locked the door and stuck the key in her pocket.

"Aren't you worried he'll scream when he wakes up?" I

asked.

She smirked. "Hasn't Mulberry taught you anything? That boy won't be conscious for at least a few hours. Chances are his friends will find him before he even realizes where he is."

"Let's get out of here then and get you to safety," I said.

She shook her head. "I can't leave those children. These men are likely to use them as leverage to get to me. If the police show up, they'll become hostages. They've already gathered most of them in the refectory."

I thought about that for a moment. "If we can lead these men into the yard, I can call in the drones. We'll mow them down with fire and brimstone before they have a chance to do anything."

"Drones?" she asked, raising an eye. "Mulberry uses those now, does he?"

"They're effective," I said.

"Things really have changed," she said. "This game just isn't what it used to be."

* * *

We reached the yard in less than a minute, the drones already on their way. They'd be here shortly, giving us just enough time to get to the shuttle, call the local authorities, and handle the remaining soldiers.

"Any idea how many there are?" I asked.

Mable glanced at the body in the middle of the yard. "Based on what you've told me, I'd say four more," she said.

"How you can be certain?" I asked.

"I saw them when they arrived from the office window," she explained.

"And you're sure you didn't miss someone?"

She raised her brow at me.

"Right, so four of them," I said. "That makes it easier."

The comm in my ear told me the drones were two hundred meters from the church but would remain elevated until the targets showed.

"Get to the shuttle," I told her, motioning to our ride. "I'll draw them out."

She looked like she was about to argue but didn't. Instead, she nodded and started jogging to the ship. Maybe she knew better than to tell one of Mulberry's people what to do, or maybe she simply trusted me enough to let me handle it. Either way, that's exactly what I was going to do.

I cracked the door to the church. "Run! Run! Hurry Sister Mable! Get out through the back! Come on!" I shouted so loud it hurt my throat, but the hollow walls would carry my voice all the way to the dining area. If this didn't work—

The second comm lit up. "They're headed outside!" barked one of the soldiers. "Get out there now!"

"I'll stay with the hostages," said another.

"Everyone else, after her!" said the first.

Three out of four would have to do for now.

I ran to the side of the building and readied my pistol after a quick magazine check. I glanced down to my waist at the smoke grenade I'd brought. Now might be a good time to use that.

As soon as the door swung open, I tossed the grenade. A large cloud formed, enveloping the men as they arrived. They coughed and shouted, rushing out into the yard to escape the fog. "Over there!" shouted the smallest of the three, pointing to my shuttle.

Now that they were out in the open, I had them exactly where I wanted them.

I brought up my pad, keying in a command to autopilot the shuttle home. The ship ignited thrusters, lifted off the ground, and began to bank away. Mable would probably be pissed about this, but I had my orders, and right now her life was the priority.

The shuttle took off into the sky and towards the eastern part of the city. It would take a while before it arrived at the garage. "Godsdammit!" yelled one of the soldiers. "Get after that ship!"

I touched my comm. "Now," I whispered.

As the three men moved toward their vehicle near the church gate, the drones descended from the sky, stopping almost a meter above the van.

The three men stopped when they saw the machines, scrambling for their weapons, but it was too late.

The drones unloaded a cascade of heat and flame on them, causing them to scream and run, fire riding their entire bodies until they finally collapsed into the grass.

Three lifeless bodies were lying in the yard, smoking and charred beyond recognition. "One to go," I whispered.

I ran inside the building, hurrying to where the last of the soldiers remained. He'd be surrounded by children. Not an easy target, to say the least.

"What's going on out there?" asked a voice in my ear. I already knew the source. There was only one person left.

I said nothing as I hurried towards the far end of the main hall, taking the first turn and nearing the kitchen. I'd come in through the back, using the counters for coverage.

I could already hear several of the younger children crying. They were scared and confused. An understandable reaction to seeing an armed group of mercenaries invade your home. Gods only knew what they'd said or done to them since their arrival.

"Shut the hell up over there!" shouted the soldier.

A loud yelp followed as the bench slid across the floor.

"Bren!" shouted a girl. "You hurt him! Bren!"

More crying followed, and this time it was even louder.

"I said shut up, all of you!"

A boiling heat ran through my throat and chest as I imagined one of the kids getting smacked around or pushed to the floor. Without even seeing it, I was already livid.

I eased my way through the door. The hinges creaked enough to make a sound, but the children's cries drowned it out. The kitchen was empty, no sign of the staff. Since the authorities had yet to arrive, I had to assume the adults were with the kids on the other side of the counter.

If only one of them had gotten out, this scenario would have unfolded quite differently.

"Is anyone gonna answer me? Ralph? Torey? Somebody?!" asked the man, his voice erupting from the dining area as well as inside the comm.

I eased my way closer to the counter. He was pacing back and forth between two long tables, children on either side of him. I could see the top of his head.

I touched the comm and cleared my throat. "Hello," I said in the lowest voice I could manage.

He stopped moving, then turned towards the other side of the room. "Who the fuck is this?!" he shouted, causing several of the kids to flinch.

Witnessing the children's fear pushed me into action. I raised myself up to my feet, extending my arm with the weapon it held and fired.

He took the bullet in his shoulder, knocking him forward to the floor where he scrambled desperately to get away.

I leaped over the countertop, gun still aimed, and the children's desperate and frightened screams were nearly overwhelming.

But at that moment, all of the noise seemed to drown itself, replaced by an empty song as total focus shrouded me. My eyes were set on the armored man with the rifle as he moved along the tiled floor. He swung his gun in my direction, but I fired twice and struck the hand that threatened to pull the trigger.

He snapped back, screaming in pain as the bullet tore his fingers apart. As our eyes locked, and I saw the fear overtaking him, I shot him in the knee, ensuring that whatever happened next, I could take my fucking time with him.

"S-stop!" he yelled, his dry voice cracking at the words.

I walked beside him, stopping when I had the barrel a meter from his forehead. "Drop the weapon," I ordered.

With one hand shaking and bleeding, he tried desperately to remove the rifle from his neck. It took him some time to do it, but eventually, he had it off. I kicked it away from both of us and then narrowed my eyes on his.

The sisters and kitchen staff were already leading the children out of the building, and before long the two of us were alone. Once I knew no one could see, I knelt beside the stranger and stared quietly at his trembling, sweating face. "You should never have come here," I told him.

"We were only following orders," he managed to say.

"Me, too," I said, placing the barrel to his forehead. "But I don't take kids as hostages."

He swallowed. "You're gonna kill me, huh? Just like you killed everyone else. Fuck you, then. Hurry up, just do it and get it over with."

I pressed the barrel deeper into him, biting my lip. I wanted to do it more than anything. He deserved it. We both knew it. No one would blame me.

The comm in my ear clicked to life. "Abigail?" asked a familiar voice. It was Pearl, and the sound of my name caused me to flinch. "Abby, are you there?"

I removed my finger from the trigger, easing the weapon back. "I'm here," I said.

"I'm outside with a team. Stay where you are. We'll be right there," she told me. "Did you take any of them alive? Anyone we can question?"

I looked down at the man before me. There was still a man upstairs, locked in the closet. I could leave him alive and we could question him, find out more about them. I had no reason to keep this one alive, except—

Clementine's face flashed before my eyes, and I remembered the way she killed that man on our first mission—sliced his throat in his own bed, and then the woman next to him. The bloodlust had grown in her like a cancer. Was I the same? Was I just like my sister?

I paused, and slowly took a step back from the trembling man at my feet. His eyes darted between my pistol and my face, confusion all over him.

I sat on the nearby bench, letting the gun dangle between my legs, all the energy in me suddenly gone.

"There's two," I muttered, letting out a sigh. "I've got two survivors."

* * *

By the time I made it home, Mulberry was already there waiting for me. He'd arrived on-world less than an hour ago. In that time, the authorities had been dispatched, and our team had long since vanished. Our government contacts would omit whatever details they needed to avoid implicating our group. Such an arrangement would require compensation from Mulberry, but given Mable's safety, I knew he was more than willing to pay.

Our team had to break into three groups, each taking an alternate, snaking path back home to escape any detection.

I had gone alone, taking a cab to the middle of the city, walking around a shopping plaza, and then using the guild's anonymous shell account, I used another public transport to travel the rest of the way. I'd asked to be dropped off a quarter kilometer from the front door. I'd made it back slightly after dark.

Mulberry went to me as soon as he saw me, and he gave me the biggest smile I'd ever seen on him.

"How'd it go?" he asked, but we both knew it was only a courtesy. He'd likely already gone over the drone footage, not to mention Mable's testimony.

I narrowed my eyes at him. "You already know how it went."

He gave me a chuckle. "I want to hear it from you. Mable said you did a fine job, but how did it feel?"

"Feel?" I echoed.

"That was your first time in the field in months," he said, honestly.

"Oh," I muttered, uncertain of what to say. The truth was, I felt exhausted, and the call of my bed tugged at me. Still, I found I was somehow happy, not only for Mable's safety and the joy I saw in Mulberry's eyes but also for the success of my mission. It felt right, every part of it. "Where's Mable?"

He frowned, but only slightly. "She's gone," he said, sighing slightly. "She said to tell you thank you, but she had to leave. If I know her, and I'd like to think I do, she'll find another church, maybe take another name. She knows the game well enough to stay out of trouble, especially after all of this."

I could hear the sadness in his voice. The knowledge that he might never see her again was ever present in the back of his throat. I knew that feeling because I felt it with Clementine.

I reached out to grip his shoulder, and I hugged the old man with all the strength I had left. "I'm so sorry," I whispered.

His arms wrapped around me, and he pulled me into his shoulder. He grunted, and I knew he meant the same.

* * *

A light tap at my door startled me awake.

I'd been reading, and I must have fallen asleep. The book was laying open across my chest, and I didn't remember putting it down. I was halfway through the second to last story in the *Tales of the Earth* book, but I couldn't remember where I'd stopped.

The mission must have worn me out more than I thought.

I checked the page number before putting the book down and standing up. I pressed the button to open the door, surprised to find Pearl standing on the other side. She looked more exhausted than I did.

"Can I come in?" she asked.

"Of course," I said, rubbing my eyes. "What is it?"

In response, she showed me the bottle and two glasses she carried before coming inside.

She put the two glasses on my bedside table and poured some amber liquid into both. She handed me one and sat down on Clementine's bed.

"So," I said, eyeing the liquor in the glass suspiciously. "What's up?"

She took a sip from her glass. "It's been a long night. Mulberry's not in the best mood, so I decided to hang out with you tonight. If you don't mind, of course."

I sniffed my glass and made a face. "What is this?"

"Bourbon. But they should have called it ambrosia, drink of the gods." She raised her glass. "Bottoms up." She downed what was left.

I took a sip and winced at the taste. My eyes bulged as the burning liquid went down my throat. "Ow. That's just terrible. How do you drink this?"

She shrugged. "It gets better after five or six glasses."

I sat down on my bed across from Pearl. "Are you drunk?"

She made a gesture with her hand. "About halfway there. I plan on going all the way tonight though if you get my meaning."

"I don't."

She shrugged and filled her glass again. "You will."

I inspected my glass and took another sip. I didn't know why I expected it to go down any better, but I was gasping by the time it went down my throat. Pearl laughed and leaned over to refill my glass.

I took another drink of the fiery liquid. "Pearl, what's Mulberry's history with Sister Mable?"

Pearl leaned back on the bed, pressing her shoulder into the wall behind her. "They knew each other before they started this place. They founded it together, I suppose you could say."

I leaned forward. "Together? I thought he built this place after she left him."

She took another sip. "Oh, yes. They were equal partners in building this place. The fact that they were in love was a separate relationship, or so they liked to claim. The rest of us knew better, though."

In love? I'd never known about that. From what little I'd gleaned by now, it was clear they'd worked together and had been friends, but to be in love was something else entirely. It redefined everything I knew about them. "I had no idea," I muttered, trying to imagine them together, making eyes at one another. "Why did she leave?"

Pearl sighed. "I don't know all the details. In those days, I spent a lot of time away, running jobs and training some of the newer recruits. Mable and Mulberry took care of the business side of things, giving out missions and targets. That's not to say they didn't still run jobs from time to time. In fact, that was ultimately the cause of why she left."

"What do you mean?"

"She killed a little girl," Pearl said, nonchalant as ever, and then took another sip of her drink. "Not intentionally, mind you, but it happened all the same. She and Mulberry took a contract on a man named Sordin Vae. They waited in his apartment, expecting him to be alone that night. He had joint custody of his daughter, but the intel said he'd be home alone that night. It was wrong, and the bomb they planted ended up taking both the target and his child out in the same, awful moment."

I said nothing.

"Everything changed after that," Pearl continued. "Mable stopped going on jobs. Mulberry started changing the way he ran the guild. Higher standards all around, no more bombs, only precision hits. He really stepped things up."

I took another sip from the glass. It still burned all the way down, but like Pearl said, it was getting easier to bear. I was feeling a little woozy, though, so I shook my head when Pearl offered to refill my glass. "Was she Number Two?"

Pearl nodded. "Still is, and she always will be, so long as Mulberry has his way."

I smiled at that.

"She left a year later," Pearl told me. "Went to that church and took her vows. It devastated Mulberry. He begged her to come home. The fact is, she was his heart. I saw it in him, just as I saw it in her. That's why she brought you girls here. Even then, after almost ten years, she only trusted him. She knew he'd protect you like you were his own daughters, because she knew the depths of his love. That's just the kind of man he is. He cares too much."

"I had no idea," I said, my eyes dropping to the floor.

"No, I don't suppose you would," she said. "Love is something for adults, and it makes them crazy and sick, all at the same time."

"I hope I never have it, then," I said, thinking that it sounded rather painful.

"Don't say that," Pearl said, and a slight smile poked through the side of her lips. "As hard as it was for him, I know Mulberry would never trade his time with Mable for anything, whether in this life or the next. She made him the happiest he's ever been. As his friend, I was glad to see him so incredibly, stupidly in love." Her eyes rose to meet mine. "And someday, Abigail, I hope to see the same in you, too."

SEVENTEEN

The alleyway was dark, and loud music from the nightclub next door vibrated through the walls. It was only a couple of hours from sunrise, but the music didn't sound like it was going to be ending anytime soon.

I crouched down in between two dumpsters, twisting the silencer on my pistol, waiting for my target.

Jeremy Breen. That was the name of the man I was waiting for. Over the year or so after I'd helped Sister Mable, Mulberry let me switch between intel and normal fieldwork.

Breen wasn't the kind of guy that our organization usually went after. Our bread and butter were thugs and self-styled kingpins. Breen's company caught him embezzling money on Crescent, in a neighboring system.

One of the CEOs—someone that apparently had a lot to lose if this came to light—sought us out to deal with him. Quietly.

He had secrets, though. The kind that the company wanted to bury, too. The kind that made Mulberry think that this was a job for me. He didn't tell me as much, but the fact that he presented the job to me personally was revealing.

A few weeks of surveillance had revealed Breen's fondness for perversion. He visited the same kind of establishments in each city he went to. We didn't usually dig into targets' vices, but the fact that each of these places had a common denominator led to a deeper study. What was revealed made me sick. It also told me why Mulberry offered me the job.

When we interrogated the owners of these establishments, each one of them agreed that Breen liked them young. Too godsdamned young. When Mulberry told me about the job, I took it. He hadn't even offered it to me yet, and I'd taken it. It was mine.

All I had to do was wait. I closed my eyes, rubbing my temples with my free hand. The music inside was starting to get on my nerves.

After another ten minutes, I heard a vehicle come to a stop just outside the alley.

I had brought a drone with me on this mission, and it was currently flying half a kilometer overhead, sending a magnified visual into my mask's eyepiece.

The man just arriving was an infamous drug dealer, Jack Reeth, also known as The Jack of Knives. He'd made quite the name for himself, here on Crescent, and he'd since become the go-to source for smuggled arms and drugs across half the planet. He wasn't my target, but he was here to meet with Breen, which opened up the possibility of clearing the streets of two problems at once. Sure, they'd only pay me for one of them, but who was I to turn down a little charity work?

I dragged the slide on my pistol back, slipping a round into the chamber.

"I have the goods you wanted, but this is way off what I usually make, Breen," Jack said. "It's going to be double the usual price. Last minute delivery fees, you know."

I could almost hear the smile in his voice.

"Fine. I don't care," Breen said, slurring his words. "Just tell me that you have enough for a party."

"Red splits, wild grass, and a few dozen Michaels," Jack said, pulling something out of a small black case, small enough to fit in his pocket. "Careful you don't get caught in there. And remember, you say my name to anyone, I'll kill ya."

Breen chuckled. "You're a good friend, Knives."

"So long as I get my money, sure," said Jack.

My knees were beginning to strain in this position, so I shifted my weight a little. In doing so, my foot brushed against the gravel. It was quiet, but loud enough for them to notice.

Shit.

Jack paused, and I could see his attention shift to the back of the alley, even from my drone's camera.

Looks like I have no choice, I thought, clutching my pistol.

I stepped out of hiding and raised my gun. I wasn't ready to kill Breen yet, but I did want his attention.

"Hey, who the hell?" asked Jack.

I fired twice, hitting him in the chest and stomach. He fell to the ground, dropping the box of drugs into a small pool of rainwater.

Breen raised both his hands. Even from this far away, I could see him shaking.

"Hey, look, man," Breen said, probably because of the mask I was wearing. "I've got money. Lots of it. Just take it and the drugs! Whatever you want!"

I tilted my head at him, keeping the weapon trained on his face. I slowly walked by him, towards the fresh body of his friend and dealer. Kneeling beside him, but still with my gun on my target, I quickly rummaged through Jack's pockets. I stowed his credits and wallet, making certain to pull out every pocket.

"Yeah, that's it, buddy," said Breen. "Just take the money and leave me alone. I barely even know this guy. You can have my cash, too!"

"Thanks," I said, getting back up. "But I'm just taking this to make it look like an amateur did this. Can't have the police thinking it was a professional, you know."

"O-oh," said Breen. "S-sure, right. You got it, man. Just don't do anything—"

The first shot ripped through his throat, making him stumble back. The second broke one of his ribs. The third splattered brains into the air behind him, all before he had a chance to put together what was happening.

I could have done it in a single shot, but that would have looked too professional. We didn't have any contacts on this planet, so things had to be done a certain way to avoid an in-depth investigation, even though the target had been a lowlife.

Maybe fortune would favor me even further tonight, and the cops would arrest someone whom Breen owed money to. There were always rivals, always someone angry at someone else.

I found the drugs and the credit chits in his pockets and pulled his pad out. The contract had mentioned this device, so I was obligated to recover it, but a small part of me wanted to toss it. The buyer would probably use this for his own end. More drugs, more deals, and more crimes.

I felt dirty at the notion of bringing it back.

I walked out of the alley and started following the main street. Rows of nightclubs and bars lit up the noisy downtown along the glistening shoreline. It was where playboys like Breen came to party.

It also made for good hunting grounds.

* * *

A lot of people didn't like space travel. Some even had valid reasons for it, but no one could deny that the view was fantastic. Slip tunnels, nebulae, and an endless sea of stars, but among them all, I had to say that seeing a slip tunnel had become a personal favorite of mine.

I still remembered the first time I'd entered one. The emerald green was so bright that it made me flinch, almost afraid of what I was seeing. I'd only heard about them in books before that, but neither pictures nor beautiful descriptions could replace the reality of their splendor. A sort of milky, flowing green, an infinite number of layers between them, and lightning from a hundred thunderstorms.

I'd heard you never got used to it, and seeing it now, I believed that was true. I couldn't imagine ever getting tired of this.

I leaned back into my seat, watching the tunnel flow by. My book was on the control panel, but on shorter trips through the tunnels, I found it was more relaxing just to sit back and watch.

A notification appeared on my screen, telling me that we would be dropping out of the tunnel in five minutes. I pulled my feet off the dash and strapped myself in.

Once the countdown reached zero, the straps dug into my chest as the transport vessel created an opening to normal space.

The comm-link pinged, an automatic hail from Ruto Port.

The ship was smaller than most, so the pilot was only a short distance from my seat, allowing me to hear every word of his response. "Port Authority, this is Shuttle AF-475, requesting permission to enter dock, over."

A pause and crackle of static. "Shuttle AF-475, you are clear for landing," the artificial intelligence returned. They never used real people for the ports if they could help it. That was only on smaller worlds, colonies, and military bases.

Entering the atmosphere took some time, but we landed without any problems. It took about thirty minutes to get through customs, but all of my papers checked out. According to the system, I was in sales, working for a company that specialized in medical equipment, grooming supplies, and lamps. Even when your corporation was fake, it was important to diversify.

A small shuttle waited for me at the port. I'd been away from the complex for a while, and even though I enjoyed my freedom more than I cared to admit, the urge to sleep in my own bed pulled at me.

"Welcome back, ma'am," said the driver, a man I recognized as Portillo. He was a year older than me, but I outranked him by twenty. Over the last twelve months, I'd shot up to Number Eleven, all at the insistence of Mulberry. I told him it wasn't necessary, but after what happened with Mable, he'd been more than insistent.

I adjusted my pad to the local time. It was nearly dinner, and the sun was beginning to set. Thankfully, I'd maintained my sleeping schedule during the trip, so my rhythm wasn't too far gone. If I could last another five hours, I'd crash and get an early start on things tomorrow morning.

As we pulled into the shuttle bay, I saw Pearl and Mulberry talking to two boys I didn't recognize. They had to be new.

Their eyes fell on me as the cab door opened, and I could tell something was up.

"Get back to work," Pearl told the boys, quickly dismissing them.

Mulberry nodded at me when our eyes met, and I stepped out of the vehicle, looking suspiciously at the two. "Didn't expect to see you down here," I admitted.

"How was Crescent?" he asked, changing the subject instantly.

My eyes narrowed further. "Lots of beaches. Busy nightlife. Lots of perverts in need of better security. How are things around here?"

Pearl stepped in to answer. "The same as usual. Contracts, surveillance, and brooding assassins." She rolled her eyes at the last part. "Oh, and you have a visitor."

I felt a tap on my shoulder, but before I could turn around, two arms embraced me, squeezing the breath out of my lungs. Her smell was all I needed.

"Oh gods," I whispered. "Clementine?"

"In the flesh!" she answered, pulling back and holding me at arm's length. "Holy shit, you've grown about half a meter since I left."

A smile broke across my face, and I was overcome with more joy than I knew what to do with. "What are you doing here?" I asked, almost balking. "I don't know what to—"

She snickered, then punched me in the shoulder, grinning. "Thought I'd stop in while I was nearby. You know, see how my sister was doing." She winked at me.

I pulled her in for another tight hug. It felt like forever since I'd seen her. She'd been gone for over a year, but it felt like a lifetime.

Pearl chuckled, tapping Mulberry's arm before turning away. "We'll give the two of you some time to catch up. Come find us if you need anything."

"I'll get you the mission brief as soon as I can," I told them, quickly.

"Don't worry about it," Mulberry responded, already at the door. "Your sister is here. Take all the time you need."

I turned back to Clementine. "What should we do? Want to go have a drink? Maybe we can—"

She shook her head. "Actually, I thought we'd hit the gym. It's been a while since we had a match. I wanna see how we stack up!"

"Of course, that's what you want to do," I told her, laughing. I took her by the hand and tugged her towards the door. "Come on! Everyone's eating, so I bet the gym is clear."

* * *

"So," I said as we took a break from sparring. "Don't take this to mean that I'm not happy you're back—because I am—but what are you doing here?"

Clem shook her head, taking a sip of water. "Well, I'm not back for good, if that's what you're wondering. I mean, I appreciate everything Mulberry and Pearl did for me—for us—but I like being my own boss. It comes with a lot of perks."

I made a face. "Sure, I get it. That does sound like a lot of extra work for the same kind of pay, though."

"Same pay?" she asked. "I don't know who you're talking to about finances, but I do pretty damn well for myself. I'm saving up for a ship right now, too. I expect to have that by the end of this year."

"Whoa!" I exclaimed.

She nodded. "Plus, I pick my own assignments and get to travel anywhere I want. I don't answer to anyone but myself. I'd say that's worth the trade-off."

I shrugged. "Another round?"

She grinned. "You know it."

We stepped back onto the mat as I put my gloves back on.

Gone were the protective paddings from our training with Pearl. We were old enough to know how to pull our punches. This was sparring, not battle. The both of us had enough of that outside this complex.

Clem advanced on me, her hands raised as she swept out a low kick, aiming for my legs. I checked the attack by twisting left, and I kept my left hand up. She always threw a hook after a low kick. When it came, I moved with it, countering with a firm jab. She blocked it, but it forced her a step back.

I tucked my chin and pressed forward, hammering a pair of body shots. She dodged to avoid them, and my right foot lashed out toward her head. Her forearm blocked the kick, but she was forced backward to recover her balance.

"Hey," she said through her mouthguard. "You're getting good at this."

"What can I say?" I raised my hands again. "I've been training every day."

"Cheeky," she said, moving in closer, but I backed away. One of the things I'd learned from Pearl was that since I was taller, I had more to gain by keeping my distance and using my longer reach to punish a shorter opponent.

"I mean," I said, keeping my guard up. "One of the advantages of having this complex is that you get to keep practicing during your downtime."

"Well lucky for me, I don't get much downtime between jobs." She tossed a couple jabs at me, followed by a wild uppercut that I barely avoided.

"You get help in researching jobs too," I said, throwing a high kick that forced her to keep her distance again. "Plus, backup when things go sideways."

"I don't need backup. I never have." Clem rushed in and tried to tackle me. I jumped to the side, pushing her back.

"Ouch," I said, only half joking.

"I didn't mean it like that," she said, backpedaling. "We worked well together. You know that as well as me. But I work well alone, too. I don't want to say that the organization was holding me back, but—"

"You're not *not* saying it."

"Exactly," she said, darting in fast with a haymaker. As I ducked under it, I realized too late that it was a feint. I saw her left leg hook around mine. It hit hard, and I dropped down to one knee.

She circled me, and before I could tuck my chin in, she wrapped her arms around my neck in a chokehold. As I fought to untangle myself from it, she groaned, leaning back and dragging me with her until we were both on the floor with her lying under me.

A few seconds later, I tapped at her arm, and she let go. I

rolled off her onto the mat, taking in deep breaths as I pushed myself up to my hands and knees.

Clem hadn't gotten rusty since she'd been gone. Like she said, even if she didn't get much training, and even if she didn't have any downtime, she could keep her skills honed while in the field. She didn't need the practice. She didn't need the support. She didn't need backup.

That stung more than it should have.

She offered her hand and helped me up to my feet.

"Only two out of three," she said with a nod. "You're better than you were, but your hand-to-hand needs work. Spend more time in the field, and you'll be throwing me around like a rag doll."

She wasn't wrong, although most of my kills came at a distance. Lately, some of that had changed, and I found myself having to adapt to various situations, all of which began with the rescue mission at the church.

I probably needed more time to grow before I could get on Clem's level.

We ran through a few more rounds on the sparring mat with Clem winning them all. I wasn't really surprised. Pearl had helped me work harder on my defense, but in the end, I lacked Clem's aggressiveness, which gave her the edge in any short-distance engagement.

I had learned over the years to stick to my strengths when

it mattered in the field, but never to give up training my weaknesses. I liked to think that it was what made me a promising young entry into the organization's field operatives.

After a quick shower and dinner, we found ourselves back in our old room.

"You remember that time where you got me to sneak under the tables in the mess hall after lunch?" Clem asked, sitting on her old bed, barely containing her laughter. "And I stayed there for three hours?"

I leaned back in my bed, grinning. "Yeah. They were looking for you all around the orphanage. Some of the nuns were wondering if you just ran away."

"And then I turned up in the dinner line—"

I laughed. "You had a *completely* straight face, holding your plate out for some food. The sisters were trying to scold you, and you kept telling them that you'd been in our group the whole time."

Clementine had to stifle a chuckle before continuing. "How did you convince the other girls to go along with that? I can't remember."

I shrugged. "I told them it was to get back at Sister Amber for giving us surprise quizzes three times that week," I explained, surprised at how easily I recalled the details. "Anyway, the rest of the girls said that you were sitting in the back of the class all afternoon. The sisters started blaming Sister Amber for negligence."

Clem leaned back in her bed, still laughing. "Oh, I'm a bad, bad person."

After a few moments of silence, I perched myself up on my elbow. "So, what kind of ship will you get?"

"I already found a scrapyard that has a couple of good ones I can start with," she said. "Nothing huge. Doesn't even have to have any weapons. I just need living quarters and a working NAV system."

I smiled. "That's pretty cool."

"Yeah, they're really expensive, though."

"How do you plan on getting the money?" I asked.

She paused, almost hesitating. "I've got a few ideas. You know me. Just some extra jobs and work I think will pay off."

I chuckled. "It has to be better than living here, sharing a tiny little bedroom with me."

She shrugged. "It wasn't so bad here, and honestly, I'd still rather be living with you. I miss having you around." She shifted her weight on the bed. "You're my sister. Not having you beside me makes it feel like I'm missing something."

I laid back on the bed, staring at the ceiling. "I know how you feel."

There was a short silence.

"That's part of why I'm here, actually," she finally said.

"Really?" I asked.

"Yeah," she said. "I mean, I still need to have a chat with Mulberry and Pearl about the actual details of it, but I have some really big plans. I just came here because I wanted you to be a part of them, Abby."

I smiled. "What kind of plans?" I asked, sitting up again. "Are you saying you want me to come with you?"

"That's exactly what I'm saying," she said, excitement in her voice. "Think about it. The two of us out on our own, with our own ship, cruising the galaxy together and doing jobs. We could be whoever we want. We could build a new life."

The thought was certainly appealing. I'd missed Clementine so much, ever since she left. The idea that we could take off together, just like we always talked about—it was like a dream come true.

Another moment of silence passed.

Finally, Clem continued. "I think we could be happy, Abby. We could find a real home."

A warm sense of joy filled me. It was almost nostalgic. I had to admit, I'd spent less time here in this bed in recent months than ever before, always opting for a long-distance mission or a reason to get away. Maybe it was all leading up to this. Maybe I was just waiting for Clementine to come back for me. Was that so bad?

Mable had chosen to leave this life and head out into the galaxy to find her own path. Perhaps that was what I needed to do, only with my sister beside me. It certainly felt like the right thing to do.

"Take some time to think about it," she said, jumping to her feet. "I know it's a lot, but there's no rush. We can go over it tomorrow."

"N-no, wait," I said, quickly, scurrying to the edge of the bed. "I want to."

Her eyes lit up at the sound of that. "Seriously?"

"Yeah!" I exclaimed, and my own excitement surprised me. "I really mean it. I think it sounds amazing. It's intimidating, sure, but I'm ready. I think I've been ready for a while now."

She smiled, then ran up to me and wrapped her arms around my shoulders. "You won't regret it," she said.

A second later, she pulled away, and she started to leave. "Where are you going?" I asked.

"I need to ask for a room," she told me.

I looked at the empty bed, then quirked an eyebrow. "What's wrong with that one? I mean, it's right here, and no one else is using it."

She shrugged. "I don't know. It's more your room now than ours. I don't want to cramp you or anything like that."

"If we're not staying here for long, why not?" I asked. "It'll be just like old times."

She smiled. "Yeah. Just like old times. I'd like that."

A few hours later, after getting Clem situated for the night, I laid back in my bed with the lights off.

Clem's breathing slowed, and I knew she'd fallen fast asleep. It was nice to have her back again, and I was surprised by how much I'd missed this. Staying in this room with her, hearing her snores as I drifted to sleep. It was all so surreal, but it felt right. She was my closest friend in all the world, and I loved her more than anything. I hoped we could be like this forever, just like she'd talked about. I hoped our future would be a bright one, full of joy and traveling, seeing things no one else had ever witnessed, living lives we never could have imagined.

We were finally sisters again, and this time, I knew things would be better.

* * *

I felt like I'd just closed my eyes when my pad buzzed insistently against my thigh. It took me a few minutes to come out of the deep, dreamless sleep I'd been in. By the time that I actually woke up, the buzzing stopped.

I groaned softly. I didn't want to wake up yet. I still wasn't fully rested.

Go away, annoying piece of crap, I thought, trying to shift around in my bed, pushing my head deeper into my pillow.

The pad buzzed again, just the one time now, telling me

that whoever had been calling had left a message. A few minutes of inner debate over whether I should check it or not, ended with a growled curse. Why couldn't people just let me sleep? I'd just gotten back from a godsdamn mission, after all.

I finally rolled over, pulling the pad out from the pocket of my cargo pants, flicking it on and letting it scan my face. It unlocked, showing a couple of failed comm links from Mulberry's go-to clean-up guy, Alec, who had an entire team under him, each of them trained by the man himself.

I was pretty certain Alec had been a forensic analyst for the Union at some point but never bothered to ask. He seemed to know more than he let on, but I supposed that was the case for most people in our line of work. Most never told anyone their full story, because too much transparency could get you killed. That was what Pearl had taught Clem and I when we were starting out, and it was a rule we'd since learned to follow.

I sighed, flipping over to the message that Alec had left me. It was in text, not voice.

The text simply read, "CHECK YOUR INBOX!!!!!"

I sighed, popping open my mail application. Sure enough, there were a handful of new files. I was tempted to just leave it for later, but the abundance of exclamation points in the message gave me pause.

Maybe I could just skim these over and go back to sleep.

Better than leaving them for later, I supposed.

The doc seemed to be a breakdown of the investigation into the attempt on Sister Mable's life. The dead guys' pads had been successfully cracked, their data dumped, and an analysis completed. Their employer appeared to be a man named Elias Hencher, a name I didn't recognize.

The file said Hencher had a brother who had been killed almost fifteen years ago by our organization. He also had a lot of military contacts, as well as connections with more than a few Renegades in the Deadlands.

He also happened to own a scrapyard on Epsy.

A list in the file laid out all the possible informants based on time of payments made and known associates. Alec was nothing if not thorough in his information digging.

One particular tag caught my eye. There was no name attached. It was for the sale of a ship in decent condition for well below the market price. The buyer appeared to have no name attached but was described as being a young woman with black hair and brown eyes.

Strange but not uncommon. She might be a Renegade or some other kind of smuggler or bounty hunter. There were plenty of people who made their way in the world anonymously, using fake names to avoid attention.

Hell, I was one of them.

I switched back over to the first file, skimming the information quickly before reaching the video feed that caught the previously referenced woman leaving the scrapyard. I played the video. The figure in question was only on camera for about two seconds. Even so, it was enough.

The woman was between 160 and 170 centimeters tall. Lean build and dressed in familiar clothes. Her long black hair had been tied up in a rigid bun behind her head.

I only caught the side of her face, but I still recognized her easily. I knew the build.

"Clementine," I whispered. "Gods, it can't be."

Was this the place she'd found her ship? Of all the people in the galaxy, why had it been this man? The same crook who'd hired that team to kill Sister Mable. This couldn't be a coincidence, could it?

I turned over to the bed beside my own, expecting to see her there, but to my surprise, she was already gone.

EIGHTEEN

Clem's empty bed wasn't an admission of guilt, but it seemed suspicious after the video I just watched. She might have only gone to the bathroom or to the kitchen for a midnight snack, but I couldn't shake the nauseous feeling in my stomach.

If her motives for wandering around the complex in the middle of the night were innocent, so be it. When I found her, I would say that I was still adjusting to recently arriving from another system and couldn't sleep. She'd understand.

The door opened with a soft hiss, and I peeked around the corners. The hallway was empty, lit only by the dim overhead bulbs.

I kept my eyes peeled as I made my way to the bathroom. She wasn't inside which troubled me, but I still needed to check the kitchen before I let my fears run rampant. Truth be told, I didn't know Clem as well as I'd hoped. She'd been gone for over a year now, which was more than enough time for someone to change. I'd assumed she'd grown into a better person since I last saw her, but the opposite was just as likely, wasn't it? After all, I certainly wasn't the same, not when I really thought about it.

Despite trying to give my sister the benefit of the doubt, I was moving stealthily through the halls like I did when infiltrating a target's home.

Several grim scenarios tumbled through my head. Maybe her story about coming to visit me was just to gain access to the complex. We hadn't spoken since our falling out. Why would she want to reconcile now?

If she wasn't here to see me, why was she here? Maybe she wanted to kill me, but if that were the case, she would have done it already. Her possible ties to Elias Hencher could mean she was hired after the others botched the job. The timestamps on the feed certainly matched the timeline.

But Mable was the closest thing to a mother we'd ever had—except maybe Pearl—so why would she go after the old nun? Was this really just about getting some money for a ship?

The kitchen was abandoned as well. Panic started building in my chest. I didn't want to believe Clem came back here to hurt anyone, but as I searched for her, old memories about previous jobs we did together resurfaced. I remembered her brutality, and the sheer joy she took in murder. I had no idea what kind of violence was still inside her now after all our time apart.

Alec certainly seemed to think she was a threat. Otherwise, he wouldn't have sent me the intel. That case wasn't something I was actively working on, so he must have known Clem was here today. Which means, he realized the danger and saw fit to warn me. No doubt, Alec sent Mulberry the exact same information, but I had to assume he was still asleep. The only reason I had seen it when I did was because I awoke in the middle of the night.

If Clem infiltrated the complex to learn Mable's whereabouts, it stood to reason we had an emergency on our hands. I needed to alert Mulberry. Thankfully, his quarters were only a short walk from here.

As I moved faster through the hall, I spotted something out of the corner of my eye. I almost missed it, thanks to the dim, evening lighting.

Down the adjacent hallway, a leg stuck out of a doorway. As I neared it, my chest contracted as the sight of a dead body took me by total surprise.

I already knew who it was. The dark, wavy hair was a dead giveaway. Alonso had a stab wound through the temple of his head.

That wasn't all. There were seven additional stab wounds throughout his torso, mostly in his stomach, but a couple in the chest.

I closed my eyes as I stood up again. I couldn't deny who was responsible for this. Nausea gripped my stomach, a deep quivering in my gut that just wouldn't let go.

"Gods, Clem," I whispered, trying to keep my panic from turning into full-blown hysteria. I had to stay focused if I wanted to stop her from hurting anyone else.

In the adjacent room, Bart had four stab wounds in his back. He was probably nearby when Clem attacked Alonso and he ran away, either out of fear or to call for help. She'd caught up to him, taken him down, and finished him off by slashing his throat. These poor fools never stood a chance.

I'd never liked either of them, but seeing them dead was something else. It didn't make me feel better about what they'd done to us when we were kids. It didn't bring any satisfaction. It was just empty and wrong, and at this moment, I felt it.

Clem had tracked some of Bart's blood on the floor, making it easier to follow her path. She'd gone in the direction of Mulberry's room, the same as me. I thought about using my comm but remembered I'd left it in my dresser drawer, and I wanted to curse myself. I was so stupid.

I also hadn't brought my gun. Perhaps that was because I knew Clem would never hurt me. She could have done that when I was asleep, but instead she'd simply left me there alone. Still, I'd let my emotions and confusion get the best of me, and I'd slipped up. It was too late to go back to my room at this point. I'd have to hurry to Mulberry.

A man's scream erupted from down the corridor.

"Godsdammit," I snapped, breaking into a sprint.

Everything was quiet now. The only sound was my heart pounding in my ears and my bare feet pattering over the floor. The trail of Bart's blood had faded, but I wasn't looking for it anymore. I was looking for another victim.

Whose body would I find?

A crack of light caught my eyes, coming from a distant door. This one wasn't in the hall but across another room. I knew that was where Galion slept, and I was drawn to go and look.

As I eased the door open, Clem's old knife-fighting instructor rested on his stomach. He was a smaller man, but he was a killer, born and bred. Clem had sliced a small yet deep cut in his lower back, right around the kidney.

Despite the surprise attack, he'd reacted in time to grab his own knife that he was still clutching in his right hand, and it had blood on it. It wasn't much, so I wasn't sure how effective his strike had been, but Clem was nowhere to be found. She likely hadn't slowed much.

Unlike Alonso and Bart, Galion's death had been quick. That much was evident. There was no hatred in it, nothing torturous in his execution. It had been precise and immediate. Almost respectful.

I paused before leaving, clenching my jaw as I took the blade out of his lifeless fingers. It felt wrong to take this from him, but I had no other choice.

My eyes ran up the rest of the hallway. A few red drops lay in the center of the corridor. Sloppy work for her, but she had to know that already. Maybe she didn't care.

The sounds of a struggle from down the hall made me pick up my pace. I was sprinting by the time I skidded to a halt at Mulberry's door.

I paused. The door was usually closed, but it hung open now with a trail of blood leading through it.

I clenched my jaw and gripped the knife tighter in my hand before stepping in closer. I heard Mulberry's recognizable growl, but breathless and in pain.

"It's over, old man," said Clementine. "Sorry to do it like this, but I need to find that woman."

Mulberry coughed before answering. "Well, you'd best kill me now, girl, because I'm not telling you shit."

My body tensed as I rounded the corner and looked into the room. Clementine stood over Mulberry, facing away from the door with a pair of bloody daggers in her hands. Mulberry was on the floor in front of her, propped up on one hand while the other covered a wound in his stomach. Blood seeped through his fingers.

Clementine laughed. "You'd sound a lot more intimidating if you weren't on the ground bleeding to death."

Clementine's eyes held their familiar manic look. Her lips curled up in a sneer, and her nose flared with quickened, frantic breaths.

She looked like a predator about to go in for the kill.

"Clem, stop!" I yelled without meaning to. All my training told me to be quiet, take her by surprise, but this was different.

I wanted to talk in an attempt to stop her, not kill her. Give her a chance to fix it and make it like it was before.

She turned around, her crazed look locking onto me. She was no longer standing over a fresh kill but facing a threat.

"Please stop," I whispered.

Her eyes shifted from mine to the knife in my hands, and she circled around to Mulberry, placing her blade at his throat.

"Drop it," she growled, scurrying behind him and holding his neck.

I reached out a hand. "Please—"

"I said, drop it!" She pressed the knife deeper, splitting Mulberry's skin. A line of blood ran along his neck and into his shirt.

My knife clattered to the floor. Mulberry narrowed his eyes at the knife before relaxing in Clem's grip.

The sight of him like this shook me more than I expected. He'd always been so strong and full of vigor, never one to submit to anyone. Ever since I'd met him all those years ago, back when

Sister Mable dropped us off, I had thought of him as unstoppable. Seeing him so helpless as Clem threatened his life, numbed me inside.

"What are you doing here, Abby?" she asked, eerily calmer than before, almost like she was a different person.

"What are *you* doing?" I asked.

"Abby," Mulberry cut in. "Get out of here. Get help. Find Pearl and—"

Clementine cut him off with a hard punch to his head. "Shut up!" she screamed. "Can't you see that I'm having a conversation with my *sister*?"

He gritted his teeth. The wound in his belly had bled through his shirt, so much that I could tell it was serious. She'd done that deliberately, no doubt to get information from him, but he'd bleed out if we didn't do something soon.

I circled around, keeping my distance as I slowly moved towards the fireplace.

Clem looked back at me, immediately relaxed. "What were we talking about?"

"You were explaining just what in the hell is going on," I said, keeping my voice low and even like I was trying to soothe a wild animal. "I'd really like to understand why you've come all the way here to do this, turning over our home—"

"*Your* home," she interrupted. "This place was never mine.

Not really."

"—and why you're killing the man that took us in," I finished without pausing at her interruption.

"Don't you get it?" she asked, scoffing. "You said it yourself, remember? You said you wanted to leave with me and get away from this place. We were never meant to live in a place like this, doing whatever this old fool told us."

"He gave us a home when no one else would. He fed us, taught us how to survive, and loved us. Look at him, Clem. That man you're killing is the closest thing to a father you or I have ever had, but you're just going to—"

She shook her head, furiously. "No, no, no! Fuck *him*! He doesn't care about us! Don't you remember what happened with Alonso and Bart? This bastard let it happen. They were going to—" She paused, swallowing. "He didn't kick them out. He didn't send them away. He just put them on some extra kitchen work and that was it! He's not a father to anyone, Abby. Fathers don't betray. They protect!"

"But he has protected us!" I pleaded. "Every step of the way, he's tried his best to help. You've just blinded yourself from it. You've—"

She laughed. "Says the girl who hasn't seen real pain. You don't know anything, Abigail. I made sure you didn't have to suffer through anything. Don't you remember? I looked after you! Me!

Not him!" She clenched Mulberry by the hair, staring down at him with wide, terrible eyes, and then she shook her head. "All that matters is our dream, Abby. Don't you want to leave with me and be free of this? We could get our own ship, and all we'd have to do is kill a few more people."

"A few more people?" I echoed, taken aback by the absurdity of such a statement. "You're talking about the only good people we've ever known! Mable and Mulberry never did anything to you. You've twisted everything in your head so you can blame them both, but the truth is, they were the only people who ever tried to help us. You could have saved your money by staying here with me. You didn't have to leave. You didn't have to do what you're doing right now!"

"Murder is murder!" she yelled. "You think you're better than me because this old man tells you that you're going after bad people? We're all bad people, Abby. *Look at us!*"

Mulberry was barely conscious. His eyelids were drooping halfway. Any second now, he was going to pass out.

Noticing my concerns, Clementine scoffed and shook her head. "He's fine. I didn't hit anything vital." She yanked his hair, forcing him back awake. "Isn't that right, you old crook? Hm?"

As Clem's gaze left me, I moved toward the fireplace's tool stand right beside me holding a brush, a dustpan, a pick, and a poker.

Clem looked at me again after nudging Mulberry back into a state of semi-consciousness. "Look, I'm sure this isn't exactly how you imagined our reunion. Neither did I really, but it's how it has to be. We're here, so let's make the best of it. Help me finish this job so we can get our ship and be free of all of this."

"Killing Mulberry and Mable shouldn't be part of that plan, Clem. You had your own career going. You could've done whatever you wanted."

She pointed at Mulberry with her knife. "Did you really think this bastard would just let me run around on my own without his supervision? They would have sent someone after me eventually. Possibly even you, thinking that I wouldn't kill you. I'm just taking action before it gets to that point. If I can score a ship in the process, why should I turn that down?"

I shook my head. "No," I said, sharply. "Mable walked away. He let her go, even though he loved her, even though she could have betrayed him later. He still did it, because Mulberry is a good and decent man. He would have done the same for us."

She laughed, sounding frantic. "You're so delusional, Abby. I know what they're about. Mulberry and Sister Mable were busy in their early days. You think what I do is bad? They did a *hell* of a lot worse." She glared down at him. "That's right. I know all about your sordid little past. I know what you've done."

I sighed, my shoulders sagging. "So, this is what you want,"

I said, quietly.

"Look, Abby, step back and think. Killing Mulberry is just a means to an end for me, but consider what we stand to gain. We'll have access to all the organization's assets. All their contacts, money, and even this complex. We can sell it or use the network for ourselves." She shrugged. "All we have to do is kill everyone here."

"Put the knives down, Clem," I said, forcing the resistance out and focusing on what I had to do. "Or I'll make you."

"Don't make jokes, Abby. It doesn't suit you," she said, rolling her eyes.

I grabbed the poker in the stand, holding it like a sword. It was still warm from the fire.

Clem chuckled. "You know I love you, Abby, but in what universe do you think you'd ever be able to hurt me?"

I gritted my teeth. "I'll do whatever it takes to snap you out of this delusion."

Clem flashed that condescending smile of hers.

"There's something wrong with you," I said. "Something that broke a long time ago. It's not your fault. It's okay. I was there. I understand it. Put those knives down, and we'll leave this place for good. I'm giving you the chance, but this is the last time."

Her smile turned into a sneer. "Go to hell and take that pathetic offer with you." She glared down at Mulberry, and her hand tensed, indicating she was about to do the thing I feared most.

I moved before I had time to think, springing towards her. She wasn't going to slit his throat like she had the others. I wouldn't let her.

I clutched the fire poker in my hand, then threw it towards Clementine like a javelin.

She yelped as it dug into her flesh with enough force to make her let go of the knife. I couldn't tell if I'd broken any bones, but the impact had been enough to give me the chance I needed to act. She had another dagger, and she wouldn't be so dramatic about trying to kill Mulberry on the second try, which meant I had to hurry.

I came in close, knowing it would give her the advantage, but reversed my strike at the last second, swinging at her head.

Clem was already dodging. She let Mulberry go, rolling away and jumping to her feet. That murderous gleam was in her eyes again, reflecting the firelight. She rubbed her arm where I'd hit it and held her other blade up.

"It didn't have to be like this, Abby," she said.

I swung the poker at her face. She leaned her head back to dodge. I backhanded another strike, hammering the poker into her ribs. This time, I heard and felt a soft crack as at least one rib broke.

She brought her arm down to trap the poker against her body, twisting to pull it out of my hand. I let it go, coming closer and hammering my elbow across her cheekbone.

Her head snapped back, but right away, I could tell I'd made a mistake. Her hand came back around, still holding a knife. I ducked down, bunching my body up, preparing for impact.

It came. I'd managed to avoid her gutting me like Mulberry, but the knife buried itself into my hip. The pain knocked the breath out of me, but it also sent my mind into overdrive.

Galion had managed to get one of Clem's knives when she'd hit him from behind. He had acted on instinct, obviously, but I needed to disarm her like he did. Somehow.

I dropped my elbow on her arm, loosening her grip on the knife and then twisting my body around. Locked in my body as the knife was, I wrenched it free from her hand and hammered my fist into her broken rib. She winced and grunted in pain, backing away.

I reached around, trying to draw the knife out. It hadn't worked out so well for Galion, but I needed an advantage. I couldn't beat Clem in an even fight.

She recovered quickly, and before I could start pulling the knife out, she roared and charged at me. I didn't move quickly enough, and she tackled me, gripping one of my thighs and lifting as she shoved. I hit the floor hard with a loud thud, gasping for breath as the impact pushed the knife deeper into my side.

Clem punched me hard in the gut. My training kicked in, and my legs caught her midsection, keeping her from mounting me.

The horrible look was in her eyes again, that manic need to kill. She'd drawn blood, and she wanted more. She was even grinning as her fists rained down on my body, knocking the breath out of me. I scrambled backward, trying to ward off her attacks. She grabbed the knife jutting out of me, yanking it painfully.

I screamed as the blade twisted, sending jolts of agony through me. I pushed her away desperately, feeling like I was going to pass out.

"Oh, no you don't," she hissed at me, trying to pull the knife out, but I reacted by kicking her in the face. Hard. The blow staggered her to her feet, stumbling backward. I turned around and tried to crawl away.

My hand connected with the hard rubber grip of a knife. I clutched it out of instinct and looked up in surprise. Mulberry's eyes locked with mine. He'd handed me the knife I'd knocked out of Clem's hand. His eyes glanced up behind me, and I turned to see Clem rushing forward, bloodlust in her eyes.

Knife in hand, I twisted around as Clem closed in on me.

A kick from her booted foot cracked a rib or two, and I winced in pain. But my hands came down around her legs, and I rolled, pulling her down with the motion. I jabbed my blade at her face but missed, and she wrapped her arms around mine, twisting around.

Godsdammit, not this again.

Her arms locked around my shoulder and elbow, twisting painfully. Her grip was like steel. I couldn't tell if she'd been holding back in our sparring sessions or if she'd gotten a lot stronger over the year that she'd been gone. Either way, my defenses were fading quickly.

I heard a loud pop, and a bolt of pain shot through my shoulder as she yanked it out of its socket. I roared in agony, gritting my teeth as I dropped the knife from my left hand.

I caught it with my right before it hit the floor.

The look of alarm in Clem's eyes almost made the dislocated shoulder worth it as I swept the dagger up with my uninjured hand and stabbed it as hard as I could into her thigh. When she wouldn't let my broken arm go, I twisted the knife into the muscle.

She screamed and let go, dragging the knife out of my hand as she pushed me away again.

"What the fuck?!" a voice screamed from the door.

Clem turned to see who it was as I twisted around to do the same.

Pearl wore a shocked expression as she tried to process

the chaotic scene in Mulberry's quarters. I turned back around toward my sister. If Clem were going to make a move on Pearl, she'd have to go through me first, and I refused to make it easy for her.

Clem didn't move. The look of bloodlust had faded into something more subdued. She stared at Pearl, the gears turning in her mind as she seemed to come to a sort of decision. Clem was wounded and winded, probably too much to stand a chance at taking down her former teacher.

Pearl went for her pistol, but in doing so, Clem reacted and began moving. My sister dashed toward the nearby window—the only one in the room. She drew a trench knife and used the butt of the weapon to smash through the glass.

She dove through the opening, shielding her face with her arms. Pearl shot off a couple rounds before Clem cleared the window, but I couldn't see the result.

We were on the second floor, and I ran to the opening to see where she landed. "She's gone!" I said, finding only an empty alleyway with shards of broken glass on the ground.

I pulled the knife out of my side, groaning softly before dropping it to the floor. Pearl holstered her gun and squatted by Mulberry.

He'd lost so much blood.

Pearl took off her green vest, pressing it into the wound in his stomach with tears in her eyes.

I'd never seen her cry before.

"You okay?" she asked tersely, looking at me from the side of her eyes.

"Yep," I answered, helping to keep pressure on the stomach wound as she wrapped up the cut on his wrist.

"Won't do much good," Mulberry said, coughing hoarsely.

"You'd better not die, you son of a bitch," Pearl said. "You stay with me, you hear?"

Mulberry ignored her, gripping my arm weakly. His fingers were cold and clammy. I looked into his old, blue eyes, and for the first time, I noticed how wrinkled and tired his face had become.

"I'm so sorry, Abby," he said, wheezing. "You were never meant to be here. You were—" He coughed again.

I clutched his hand, trying to rub some warmth into his trembling fingers. "Come on. Just stop."

He smiled. "I'll do whatever I damn well please." Another cough. "I picked Clem out for this life. I saw how she was, even back then, and I tried to help her. I tried to cage what was inside of her. It wasn't her fault. She'd had a rough go of things. But she saw enemies in everyone, including her friends."

I knew Mulberry was right. Clementine had lived for so long in pain. She'd found a way to channel that into something she could use, but in doing so, lost herself to it. In that time, she had protected me from that same torture, always seeking to save me, but now I'd thrown myself in front of her and rebuked her offer of freedom. *She must think I hate her*, I thought. She must feel so betrayed.

But the impulses overtook her. The need for violence burned her insides apart. "I see the pain in your eyes, Abigail," continued Mulberry. "But this is not your fault. It's mine. I failed her, and I failed you. I'm so sorry, poor girl. I ruined both your lives."

He coughed again, and blood flecked his lips.

"We need a fucking medic," Pearl said into her comm for what had to be the third time in as many minutes.

Mulberry gripped my hand again with what little strength he still had. "Leave this place behind. You deserve better than us. You deserve to be happy."

"Stop," I whispered, hot tears streaming down my cheeks. "Don't be so dramatic, old man. You heard Miss Pearl. She'll kill you if you die."

Pearl swallowed but said nothing.

"If you see Mable again, tell her I love her," Mulberry continued. "Tell her I'm sorry. I was a fool. I should have left this life behind when she did. I should have—" His voice started to fade. "I should have...taken her away, like she asked. I should have..."

I held Mulberry's hand as his grip loosened, all the strength of a great man evaporating before my eyes, and there was nothing I could do to stop it.

"Mulberry? Mulberry!" Pearl turned away from her comm, shaking him for a response.

I couldn't say anything. I let his hand go and sat back on the floor, my eyes staring ahead, my mind empty and cold. I couldn't speak. I couldn't move.

I could only watch as he slipped away.

NINETEEN

"Good gods," the voice said through my comm. "You know what time it is?"

I kept my eyes on the road ahead of me. "Obviously Pearl hasn't filled you in on the situation."

He paused as I merged onto the highway.

"What happened?" Alec asked, his voice going more serious.

"Clementine happened," I answered, simply. "She took out Mulberry and three others, including Galion."

I could hear him start to say something, but then pause, processing everything. I knew that feeling all too well. "I thought she was just a snitch. I never imagined she'd go this far. I should have called Mulberry's emergency line when I saw the footage from that salvage yard. I can't believe how stupid I was. I—"

"Stop it. There's no time to feel guilty. You want to fix this? Then help me find Clementine," I said, letting that chilly fire in my stomach dampen the emotion from my voice. "What happened is nobody's fault but hers. She got away, but she's hurt. Pretty badly, too. I need you to get to work, Alec. Right away."

He cleared his throat. "I'm already at my screen."

"Good," I said. "She stole one of the shuttles on her way out. I'm assuming she turned the tracker off, too. Is that right?"

A short pause. "Looks like it."

"She doesn't have much of a lead," I told him. "And she'll need to stop somewhere soon. Probably won't leave the planet yet. She needs to patch those wounds. Pearl's already talked with our contacts at the local precinct, so we'll know if she's flagged. Are there any transports headed out soon?"

"I have a few listed for departure later tonight, but nothing for a few hours, at least," said Alec.

"That gives us time. She likely has her own contacts, maybe someone to fix her up."

"I'm not seeing anyone admitted into a hospital with knife wounds fitting her description. Where was she stabbed?"

"In the thigh," I explained. "But I doubt she'll go there."

"I'll keep an eye on it anyway. You never know when we might get lucky." Alec sounded fully awake now.

"In the meantime, use the registry to track all outbound tickets at both major ports. The facial recognition software should be able to tag her as soon as she tries to leave."

"I'm already on it," he told me.

* * *

It didn't take long for Clem's face to pop up on the system, pulled by a local security camera in a neighboring area. Not long afterward, Alec pulled a ticket with her face on it, purchased remotely and by someone else. In the image, she'd changed her clothes, cut and dyed her hair, and changed her eye color. Not bad for someone with a knife wound, and it had only been a few hours since I'd seen her last.

I stared at the picture, which had the name Juliana Dyne under it. I'd never heard of that alias before, and I barely recognized Clementine in the image. Her skin looked a few shades darker, her lips a little more lush and red. In the time since we'd gone our separate ways, she'd gotten better at blending in. I had to give her that.

"Who bought this ticket for her?" I asked.

"Looks to be a Jared Vera. He purchased it using his personal holo, but the picture is hers. The system requires it," he explained.

"When does the shuttle leave?"

"In four hours," he said. "I have a home address for Vera if you're interested."

The address pinged from my comm to the HUD. I was already headed in that direction, based on the last available camera footage from that neighborhood. "What can you tell me about him?"

"He's former Conference. He was a member of Jodie Crom's section of the cartel. When Crom died, he disappeared and went into business for himself."

"I thought he sounded familiar," I said.

"Yep," Alec said, sounding distracted as he dug furiously into the man's life. "Not married. No children, and lives in an apartment alone in the lower east side, near the docks. About ten minutes away if you hurry."

I sighed, leaning back into the seat. "I'm on my way."

I gripped the controls. It was hard to focus. So many feelings rushed through my mind. If I failed, I'd probably never get a second chance to stop her. She'd go after Mable, and that would be the end of it. She'd kill the woman who'd saved us, and I couldn't let that happen. My own feelings about Clementine didn't matter anymore. I would always love her, but I couldn't let her do this.

I took a deep breath, trying to silence the voices in my head. One thing at a time. I had something to do now. Someone to go after. I wasn't just flailing helplessly at the universe.

Focus, Abby, I told myself. *You have a job to do.*

* * *

I took a few minutes to case the building. It didn't need much more.

I'd grown so used to targets that had extensive security systems. If they didn't have guards on the ground, they had alarms at every entrance. Fortunately, I'd been trained to deal with all of them.

In this instance, the building had several hidden cameras located along each of the outside walls. They were military-grade, suggesting they likely belonged to Vera. After all, considering the state of the building, it stood to reason the owner probably didn't care much for upkeep.

Vera had chosen this place because of that, but he also needed to ensure his own safety. That was fine, I supposed, but it wouldn't keep me from my target.

Alec used his government security codes to break into the network in under five minutes, disabling all cameras around the building. If Vera and Clem were inside, not only would be unaware of my location, but we'd be able to monitor their movements, using their equipment.

The lower east side wasn't the most welcoming part of the city. The apartments were rented mostly by dock workers who spent the better part of their time on the water, whether that included fishing, packing seafood, or loading the hauls into crates and shipping them out.

Maybe that was why the building was so empty. With everyone out to sea for the season and considering the time of day, there was no one around to get in my way.

I found the apartment quickly, and while the door was locked, I managed to use my pad to emulate the right RFID frequency, unlocking it with little effort. As the door eased open, I held my pistol at the ready and took my time checking the corners. Doorways were kill zones, which meant you had to go in slow and tight.

The single bedroom apartment that greeted me was less than impressive. It wasn't a terrible place to live, but it had a rotten smell to it. Cigarette smoke had stained the walls and turned the carpet yellow.

I couldn't imagine Vera was happy here. Maybe that explained his helping Clementine. She probably offered him a decent amount of credits to get her that ticket.

I hugged the wall and moved quietly through the apartment, sweeping every room as I moved. When I finally found Vera, he was face-down in his bed and covered in blood.

She'd killed him and left the body behind.

I cursed, mostly at the time I'd lost coming here. I could've gone to the port and waited for her there, but I was hoping to avoid the civilians. "Alec," I said, touching my comm.

"Let me guess," he began. "She's gone."

"And Vera is dead," I added.

He sighed, letting it linger in my ear for longer than I cared to hear. After a few seconds, he cleared his throat. "Should I deploy the drones to search the city?"

"Do it," I said, checking the room before leaving. There was nothing here, and I didn't have time to run a more thorough search. Not that it would make a difference. I knew where Clem was headed, so all I had to do was get there first.

"Understood," he responded. "I'll have a few head to the port, too."

"Anything out of the ordinary," I told him. "Report it all."

* * *

As I walked to the building entrance, the sun broke through the window and I paused. I couldn't just run outside. Gods only knew whether or not Clementine considered me a threat. She killed Vera and might be waiting out there with her rifle trained on me. Then again, she always favored a more personal touch—blades and strangulations. A more personal kill. I wondered, would she be so brutal to her own sister?

A small boy rode his bike down the nearly empty street. We locked eyes, but he kept going, heading into an alleyway—the one directly beside Vera's building.

"Anything from your angle?" I asked into my comm.

"Nothing yet," said Alec. "Still looking."

I let out a short sigh, thumbing the butt of my pistol, getting antsy. I opened my mouth to ask Alec the same question once again, but he cut me off.

"Hold on," he said, and I could sense he was looking at something. The words lingered on the comm for a few seconds. "Huh."

"Will you just tell me already?" I asked.

"That boy on the bike," he said.

"The scooter?" I asked.

"Whatever, yes," he replied. "He's doing something."

"People tend to do that," I said.

"It looks like he's taking a duffle bag from behind the dumpster," Alec said. "He's also talking, but there's no one else around. Must be a comm."

I tilted my head. It wasn't unusual for a boy his age to have a communicator. "What's he doing with the bag?"

"It's over his shoulder, and he's back on the scooter. Looks like he's leaving. Want me to follow?" Alec asked.

"Do it," I said. "It could be nothing. Cartels use kids for this sort of stuff all the time, but it could be—"

"Clementine," Alec finished.

I ran to the other end of the hall, towards the rear exit. This one led into another alley, which would take me around to where the boy was leaving. I'd have to keep my distance, but the drones could watch his movements from afar.

"I'm moving outside," I said, easing the back door open. A stench like sour bread and rotten cheese, struck me in the face and made me flinch. The boy would be a block away by now, which was far enough to follow safely, thanks to my eyes in the sky.

I pursued him for nearly ten full minutes before Alec told me to stop.

"Wait a second," he said, once I'd gone about six city blocks from the apartment building. "There's a ground transport. He's running up to the driver's side with the bag."

I hurried around the corner and pulled out my scope, trying to get a clear view.

I quickly withdrew my rifle from my back. I trained my scope on the boy, trying to get a good look at him.

The boy tapped at the window, saying something that I couldn't hear. From the look on his face, I guessed he was asking for money. The window rolled down, and a gun came out from inside, pointing at the kid's head. He raised his hands, fear washing over his preteen face.

I watched him hand over the bag.

That was when I saw her.

Clem leaned out the window, her dark hair catching the first few rays of sunlight.

My heart hammered in my chest, and my mouth went dry.

I still wasn't sure I could kill her. I could see her face now, profiled in my scope. She had that same manic look about her. I always used to think that it was a façade she put on when she needed to intimidate someone. Maybe that was still true, but she wore it so often, I was beginning to think the other side had been the mask and *this* was the true Clementine.

I gripped the rifle tighter, watching the scope tremble slightly.

Don't even think about it, I told myself. *Just squeeze your finger a little bit more. Kill her. End this. Don't let it go on.*

I closed my eyes, feeling a warm tear run over my cheek.

And I pulled the trigger.

The rifle boomed, jumping hard into my shoulder. I sucked in a breath as I trained my scope down to where I'd shot, spotting a smoking hole in the hood of the cab.

The shot sent the nearby bustling crowd into a wild panic as they fled and scattered.

The engines failed with a loud cough and backfire, and the vehicle stalled on itself, going dead. The kid had ducked down, covering his head and screaming for help. Clem was looking up, scanning the street. Seeing me, she pointed her gun up.

I exploded away from the corner of the building just in time as three rounds clipped the concrete where I'd been standing a second before.

She'd returned fire in a hurry, and while she wasn't bad

with a gun, the distance between us was too great. Meanwhile, I still had a chance at tagging her and ending this.

She exited the vehicle, coming around to catch up with the kid who had been trying to get to the other side of the car. Before I could reload the chamber, she punched the boy in the gut as he doubled over, and then she brought him around between us, using his body as a shield.

I cursed under my breath, but reloaded the chamber and focused on the scope. I could still hit her, even with the boy in the middle.

She ducked behind the child, then chaotically and frantically fired in my direction.

Rounds whizzed past me, but I didn't look up from my scope. She slowly worked herself away from the ruined shuttle, backing up towards one of the nearby office buildings owned and operated by the docking company.

I aimed just a little high and shot again. I wasn't going to risk hitting the kid just to kill her, but if she panicked, she might make a bad move and start running for the building without her hostage.

She ducked again, looking at where I'd hit and then back at me. I fired another shot, grazing both their heads, purposefully too high, but she didn't react this time. She just inched toward the building, holding the crying child in her hands. When she got close enough, she turned around and shot out the glass doors.

I watched her closely as she disappeared into the building, dragging the kid along with her.

"Fuck," I growled, pulling away from the scope.

I'd had my chance, and in a moment of weakness, I'd blown it. She had to know that.

I resisted the urge to throw my rifle on the ground in frustration but didn't take the time to disassemble it either. I set it behind a dumpster and sprinted for the door.

Clementine would kill that boy. I could sense it coming. It wouldn't matter if I let her go or gave her space, she'd end his life simply because he'd seen her face. Not to mention the people in the building and the street. She'd kill anyone who got in her way, and she'd keep on doing it for the rest of her life. It was all she knew—the only way she could survive.

That was why I couldn't stop chasing her because she would keep on hurting people for as long as she drew breath. I'd have to kill her. It was the only way.

I reached the stairwell, the child's screams echoing through the building from several flights above. I started moving, taking two steps at a time, going as fast as my feet would allow.

It wouldn't be long before the authorities arrived. With all those people outside screaming in confusion, someone was bound to connect what happened. I didn't have much time.

I rolled my shoulders and pulled my mask on. If this was how she wanted to play it, fine. I'd give her the fight she so desperately craved. I'd end this whole thing once and for all.

For Mulberry and Pearl, but most of all, for me.

* * *

Three flights up from the ground floor, I found the body of a short, pudgy man in a guard's uniform. Older with a balding head and white hair, he'd fallen in the same way Mulberry had when he died, and a sudden flash ran through my mind of the old man in those final moments.

I let out a bitter sigh, stepping over the body, trying to push the images out of my head. Instead, I clutched the pistol in my hand even tighter, hurting my fingers.

Several floors remained, but the next one had drops of blood right outside the open doorway. Was it Clementine's? Was she still hurt from the fight in Mulberry's room? I wondered if, in all the chaos, her wound had torn itself open again. If so, it explained her panicked behavior. She was like a cornered animal, desperate to survive. That also meant she was more dangerous, ready to do anything to get away. I wouldn't be able to anticipate her actions, because she wasn't thinking clearly.

The hall ahead of me had dark, grey carpet. Light from the distant windows beamed through, giving the area a soft, unsettling ambiance.

I slowed my pace, keeping my gun up as I circled around the corner. My eyes hadn't adjusted, but I couldn't stop moving. The longer I waited, the more time Clem had to find an exit.

I couldn't see a fire escape yet, but there had to be one somewhere.

One of the office doors stood open, and I raised my gun as I approached. This seemed too obvious. Even if she were injured, Clem would know to cover her tracks better than that. I moved closer, coming down to a crouching walk.

The boy was sitting on the floor inside with his hands covering a wound in his stomach. Tears covered his face. Confused and panicked, his lips trembled as he struggled to breathe with a horrified look in his eyes.

"Shit," I said, sweeping the rest of the room before heading over to him.

"I-it hurts," he said softly, gritting his teeth. "P-please, h-help me."

I pressed a gloved finger to his neck, feeling his pulse. It was quick but steady. I might still be able to save him.

I knew why Clem did this. She could have killed him, but she left him here for me to find. She wanted me to save him because it would mean letting her go.

I pulled gauze from my pouch and pressed it into his stomach. "Keep pressure on it. You're going to make it through this, kid."

He gasped, trying to smile. "Are you a cop?"

"No," I said. "Where's your comm? We need to call the police to come get you."

"She took my comm," he said softly.

I pulled my mask up enough for me to reach my own comm, and I pressed it into his ear. "Use mine. Call them." I unlocked the security on the device to allow the police to track it, which would lead them directly to the boy.

He nodded, placing the comm in his ear.

I wanted to stay with him and help, but I couldn't let Clementine get away. If I didn't stop her now, she'd kill more people, and there'd be no end to any of this.

After he made the call to the police and told them his location, I asked him to stay put. "I'll come back here soon, but if the cops show up, you go with them. Understand?"

"O-okay," he said, quietly. "But who are you?"

I reflexively opened my mouth to say my number but stopped. "I'm Abigail," I said, honestly. "What's your name?"

"Arin," he replied, giving me a gentle smile.

I returned it. "See you soon, Arin."

I turned and jogged back to the stairs, pulling the door open. Clem could have already escaped, but I had to take the chance that she was still here.

Shuffling steps echoed through the stairs from far away. She was running, and there was desperation in her movements. I peeked over the railing of the stairwell, only to be met by gunshots. They ricocheted off the metal beams and railing.

Gunshots made me jump back. They were from *above*. I raised my weapon and fired in return when I saw movement. Maybe in her rush to get to the top, she hadn't realized just how ingenious her plan was until it was too late. She must have doubled back since she was only five floors above me.

She was too far into the stairwell for my line of fire, but I could hear her running up the steps. Impressive, considering her wound. Then again, this was Clementine. She'd always pushed beyond her limits.

I raced up the stairs, closing the distance between us. She seemed to be heading to the roof, possibly for the fire escape, but I'd catch her before that. At her current pace, she couldn't outrun me. Not with those wounds.

A couple wild shots hit the stairs beside me, pulling me back closer to the wall.

Below us, doors opened and boots shuffled. The police were here, no doubt, which gave me little time to finish this job.

The door next to me said twelve. They'd have to climb all the way to us, but if I just kept moving, I could stay ahead of them.

Even so, we didn't have much time left. I supposed Clem getting locked up was better than her continuing. It would certainly be better than having to kill her myself.

Then again, I'd be arrested as well, and knowing Clem, she'd take her own life before she let anyone take her to prison. The last thing she'd accept was living out the rest of her days in a mining colony on some other world.

Clem must have heard the police, because she stopped shooting at me, opting to run instead. We had another ten or so floors to go before we reached the top. I followed her lead, giving the climb everything I had.

To her credit, Clem managed to keep pace with me all the way up, staying about two floors above me before she opened the door to the roof. I made my way there, gasping for air as I finally neared it. Sweat soaked into my suit as I paused in front of the door.

The stairs ended. This was as far as we could go.

I gripped my gun tighter, trying to ignore the sound of my heart pounding in my ears. I gulped down another lungful of air before pulling the door open.

It was a maintenance area with a water pump straight ahead of me along with the pulley system for the elevators. There weren't any lights on, and I could hear machinery working. It was warm and dark, and the air had the taste of rust in it.

Was Clem still running? She had to be as tired as I was, if not more.

Gunfire echoed in the darkness, and I ducked, raising my pistol. My breathing and heartbeat had been so loud before this, but now they were gone, replaced by the moment.

There was only one way through the room, and that was forward. I tried to stay quiet, moving slowly towards the other side.

A trickle of sweat ran down the small of my back. It felt like someone was watching me, waiting for my guard to drop before slashing my throat open and ending it all in a sudden, brief exchange.

I pictured Clem's manic eyes. I imagined her standing over me, bloody knife in hand as I choked on a river of blood. She would lean down and stroke my hair, and that terrifying smile would be the last thing I saw.

I shook my head, pushing that cold feeling of dread from my stomach. I needed to finish this. One way or another, it would end today.

Before I made it halfway through the room, something hit me hard in the side. Clem grabbed my hand holding my weapon. I fired, but the bullet soared off into the darkness, far away from us. She jabbed me in my ribs. My suit absorbed some of the force, but she knew the design well enough to get most of the pressure through.

I gasped, spit bursting from my mouth.

She twisted around, striking me in the jaw and throwing my head back. White pinholes of light filled my vision as she pushed me back into a wall. The impact drew a pained grunt from me as I felt my suit tense.

She shoved her forearm against my throat, leaning her full weight into it. I coughed hoarsely, trying to breathe. Tears welled in my eyes, and I reached out, fingers pressing into her face, searching for her eyes. As my fingers found her lashes, she pulled away, lessening the pressure to my neck.

As she did, I took the opportunity to lunge at her, trying to jab her in the throat. She leaned back to dodge the strike, and I brought my leg up to her stomach.

Making contact, she yelped an awful cry while still holding my wrist. Still keeping my gun away from her, I started pushing back. We both fell to the floor, clumsily rolling on one another, and she finally let my weapon go. She sprang to her feet, kicking at my hand, but I moved in time to fire.

She reacted instantly, dodging clear of my aim. I pulled the trigger again. My eyes were teary, and I was coughing hard. I wiped my sleeve across my forehead and blinked, trying to see where she'd gone.

Even so, I kept pulling the trigger until the gun clicked

empty. By the time my vision cleared, Clem was gone, and I was still prone on the floor.

I coughed again, lifting my mask to spit the accumulated phlegm from my throat. I ejected the empty magazine and put my last one in.

Like Pearl said—if you needed more than three mags, you were doing it wrong.

I chambered a round, rolling my neck as I pushed myself back to my feet. Everything hurt. It was hard to breathe, and it felt like something might be broken.

I bit my lip and swallowed a dry throat.

"Of course, there's a ladder," I muttered as I reached the far side of the room, looking up to where the sunlight pierced the dark through the cracks of the hatch in the ceiling. I started climbing. Each rung led to a new part of my body screaming in pain, but I ignored it.

I pushed the door open, pausing for a few moments before raising my knife to use as a mirror, angling it to see what was around. When I was satisfied, I stepped outside. A gust of wind caught my dry eyes, and I instinctively took a deep breath of the fresh air through my mask.

I tapped my ear, hoping to call in a few drones to check the ceiling, but it was gone. I'd given it to the kid. Gods, this just wasn't my day.

A foot kicked me in the side of the face, knocking my mask off. A knife dug into my shoulder. It was a shallow cut, but the pain made me cry out. I squirmed out of the hatch, rolling away and grasping the hilt of the knife.

I managed to twist around. My side ached so badly that I felt sick as I twisted the gun toward Clem's head and pulled the trigger. I missed, wavering on my feet as my shoulder burned with the pain of the fresh wound.

I pulled the trigger again, trying to point the barrel back at her. She came in close and gripped the gun, holding it above our heads, trying to wrestle it free from me, but I wouldn't give it up. I couldn't.

My free hand jabbed into her injured ribs, and I tried to gain control. I shot, again and again, hoping to throw her off balance, but she refused to flinch.

That was when the gun clicked empty for the third time.

"Looks like you're all out, Abby!" she snapped, a wicked grin etched across her face.

I pressed my knee into her gut and shoved her away. She staggered, clutching her bleeding side, and I rolled to my feet. She did the same, and we stared at each other, taking a second to recover.

Finally, I reached for the only weapon still remaining which was the combat knife on my hip.

Clem pulled two more daggers from her belt, spinning them neatly. "You're just so determined. I have to say, I'm impressed."

"You killed Mulberry," I said, lifting my hands and readying the knife.

Clem laughed. "We both know I'm better at this part. You've lost your only advantage."

I shrugged. "Prove it."

She nodded, also raising her hands up in a fighting stance.

We stared at one another for a long moment, the air thick and cold as I tried to steady my breathing. Our eyes locked, and I knew there was no going back.

She lunged at me, and then again. When her hand came close, I tried to sweep her wrist with mine. She pulled back, avoiding it.

Her knives arced through the air. All of Galion's training was on display, and it was all I could do to block and evade the first flurry of attacks. I slipped past her and stabbed at her arm, slicing into her flesh. She didn't scream but only stepped away as blood seeped through her sleeve and onto her hand.

I felt a sting on my arm where she'd cut me. I hadn't noticed it in the heat of the moment, but it was there.

I stepped forward, and she reacted by swinging her knife, only to pull back and sweep her other hand toward me. The blood from her wound spattered across my eyes, blinding me. I staggered away from her, swiping my knife frantically as I tried to wipe it off.

I couldn't see the next attack, but I certainly felt it. Her dagger plunged into the thin layer between my left breast and shoulder. I shoved her away from me, but she'd already split the armor. Thankfully, it had only nicked my skin.

She grunted, furiously, and I responded by coming in close to her and wrapping my arms around her chest. She dug her knife into my shoulderblade, but the armor was thick enough to keep it from piercing my skin, though I still felt the pain and pressure.

Before she had a chance to try again, I pulled my head away from her, looked her in the eye, and brought my forehead down into her nose. There was a tremendous crack as my skull collided with the cartilage of her nose. Her head snapped back with blood flowing over her lips as she staggered back a few steps.

I gripped my knife tighter, watching as she wavered from the blow.

Blood dripped down my fingers, and I swayed, trying to raise my hands again.

She raised her blade and swung. I moved to avoid it, leaned down, and aimed a punch for her wounded thigh. Her knife arced down, looking for my neck.

I froze, stopping my attack and withdrawing slightly,

letting her blade pass by a few centimeters.

I grabbed her wrist, dragging her around with every ounce of strength still in me.

She stumbled, losing control of her momentum.

I slipped my fingers beneath hers and pried the knife out of her grip, plunging the blade into her abdomen. She let out a shriek of pain like nothing I'd ever heard.

The fight had taken us right to the ledge. She turned, her heel catching the raised stonework, and she lost her balance.

I caught her by the collar. A look of shock covered her pretty features.

I dragged her back from the brink, and as she fell into my arms, the butt of the knife in her belly sink further in as it pressed against me.

I felt, rather than saw, all this in Clem. She wrapped her arms around me out of instinct from the fear of falling. Then she stiffened, gripping me tighter until she suddenly went limp, dropping to the ground.

I held her close, gently lowering her to the damp stone.

She raised a weak hand, trying one last time to swipe at my throat with her fingers, but she couldn't even lift it halfway to me.

"Abby," she said, her voice shaking.

"I know," I whispered, sitting next to her, leaving the knife buried in her stomach.

"I can't believe you—" She swallowed, and I could see blood inside her mouth. "—killed me. I can't believe you killed me."

Tears filled my eyes. They were thick and ready like they'd been waiting to burst out of me all day. Maybe they had.

"All I—" She swallowed. "All I wanted—you were all I wanted, Abby. I just—"

"But you had me," I whispered, stroking her dark hair. "Don't you remember? I was right there beside you."

"N-no," she muttered, her eyes distant and cold, flicking between invisible, distant things. "You turned on me. I tried to protect you—always tried to protect you—but you were the same as everyone else. Neither of us had a choice with our lives. The orphanage, and then Mulberry. They put us in cages and called it kindness. I—"

We were—we were slaves. You—You didn't see it, but— but I saw it. I knew."

"It's okay now, Clem," I whispered, the strain in my throat growing too tight, even as I said the words. "Just let go of those things. They don't matter anymore."

A tear ran from her eye and down her cheek. Her fingers tensed and relaxed, and I could see a lifetime of pain and fear on her. She'd kept it inside for so long, always pretending to be strong. Always putting on a show. But here in this moment, I saw the same girl from my childhood, the same innocent child I'd called my sister.

She let out a final sigh, her tired eyes finally relaxing into a quiet, still expression.

"I'm so sorry," I said as the grief overtook me, and all at once, I felt the weight of my whole life bury me. I wanted to die with her. I wanted to be free.

I was alone now, trapped in this world without her, and all at once, I was afraid.

TWENTY

A professional killer could never assume that their target was going to be an easy mark. Every mission had an innumerable number of variables that could never be fully accounted for. Sure, plans were put in place and precautions were taken, but once the proverbial shit hit the proverbial fan, the best professionals were the ones who knew how to improvise.

I slipped into the crowd, my eyes on the target. I wasn't wearing my armor. As inconspicuous as it was, it would be noticed in a crowd like this. With so many people together, one of them was bound to bump into me and feel the armor react to them.

In this case, anonymity was the best defense.

Besides, it wasn't like I was expecting a fight. If all went well, I'd be in and out before anybody noticed I was there.

I slipped through the crowd, gently pushing forward faster than the others around me. I wasn't in a rush. I needed to advance through the crush of people while remaining part of it. Step by step, I kept my eyes down but always tracking my target, moving closer and closer, inching forward until I was less than ten meters away.

Five meters.

Two meters. I was still behind. She couldn't have noticed me. I reached my hand out.

An iron grip on my wrist stopped me dead in my tracks.

"Did you really think you could sneak up on me, Abby?" Mable asked, turning around.

"I've got to stay sharp," I answered, smiling broadly and wrapping my arms around her.

We moved out of the flow of people, who were already looking at us in annoyance, and stepped into a nearby cafe. We found a table. I asked for a coffee and a plate of breakfast, and Mable did the same.

"You look good," Mable said, her eyes very serious. "I heard what happened with Clementine. I'm sorry."

I nodded, but said nothing.

I absently ran my fingers over the wound in my shoulder. It had healed, but the memory was still fresh.

"How're you holding up?" she asked.

"Well, the doc gave me some meds, patched me up, and sent me on my way after a few weeks. I used the time to track you down. Alec helped with that."

She nodded, and the server returned with our orders. A

few moments of silence passed.

"Why are you here, Abby?" she finally asked.

I swallowed a piece of meat, then washed it down with some milk. "Mulberry asked me to give you a message when he died."

"Did he?" she asked.

"He said—" I paused, surprised at the sudden lump in my throat. "He said to tell you he was sorry. He wanted you to know he loved you more than anything, and he should've gone with you, all those years ago. That was it, I think."

She stared at the table for a few seconds, a familiar, tender smile taking shape across her face. It was the same one I'd seen all those years ago, back in the orphanage. The same simple joy she'd shown to everyone who would see, and then again when she'd brought us to Mulberry. "Did he?" she asked, nostalgia in her voice. "That much, I do believe."

We ate together for a few minutes before either of us spoke again. We had known each other for so long but had been separated for most of it. Still, we shared so much with one another, between our professions and the people we knew. Mulberry, Clementine, Pearl, and all the others in the guild and the Church. I loved this woman, and I knew that she felt the same about me.

"I never wanted that life for you, you know?" asked Mable.

"You needed to leave the orphanage, and his was the first name that came to mind. You were only supposed to work there until he found you a better place. One thing led to another and—"

"I know," I said, feeling my voice cracking as I stared into the coffee cup. "He saw something dark in Clem. I was just there for the ride. If I'd never joined her, I never would've been there at the end. Maybe things would have been—"

"Don't do that, Abby," she said, placing her hand on my arm again. "What happened that night was Clem's fault and nobody else's. She broke a long time ago. Maybe Mackavoy did it to her. Maybe it happened before we ever knew her. Only the gods know for certain, and I suspect they'll never tell."

"That's what Pearl kept telling me," I said, keeping my voice low. "Someday, maybe I'll believe it."

Mable smiled and leaned over to stroke my hair. "So, where are you going now?"

"Mulberry's last wish was for me to leave this whole life behind. Honestly, I'd been toying with the idea myself. After everything, I don't think I can just go back to it. Too many memories." I let out a sigh. "Maybe I'll travel around, find something that I love, and do that. The universe is a big place, right? There has to be something out there for me."

Mable chuckled. "I'm glad you're leaving that place behind you. Finding something that you love is always more fulfilling."

I tilted my head. "Is that why you became a nun?"

She shrugged. "There were other elements to my choice at the time. Penance mostly, but over the years, I found myself caring for the children more than worrying about paying for my past sins. I didn't know it, but finding you and the other girls were the greatest joy in my life." She blinked, her eyes suddenly distant. "That, and being with that man."

We finished our meal, then stood from the table, and I wrapped my arms around her, holding on to the moment for as long as she'd let me.

"I'm going to miss you," I whispered, leaning back to look at her. "Where are you going from here?"

"I think it's best if you don't know," Mable said softly. "I'm going to disappear. Even with Clementine gone, there are plenty of people in this universe that want me dead. I can't afford to stay in one place for very long."

I nodded, but it still broke my heart.

"In that case, I hope to run into you sometime in the future, Sister Mable," I said.

"Me too, dear." She stroked my cheek. "Goodbye for now."

She turned around and walked out of the café. I considered leaving, too, but brushed a tear from my cheek and took a seat instead.

I sipped at my coffee. "You didn't have to sit all the way

over there, you know."

Pearl looked over from the table in front of me. "I didn't want to ruin the moment."

I shrugged. "It's okay. I'm pretty sure she knew you were there anyway."

"Probably." She stood up from her table and joined me at mine.

"So," I began.

"So," she said.

"Babysitting me?" I asked.

"More or less," she said, tilting her head. "You left without saying a word to anyone. I had to find out where you were by interrogating Alec."

"Poor guy," I said.

"Trust me, he's fine," she assured me. "I mostly just wanted to let you know we're dissolving the guild."

"Oh?" I asked, only partially surprised by the idea. With Mulberry dead, it certainly made sense. He was the backbone of that entire operation.

Pearl shrugged. "I'm retiring. Without Mulberry around, it'll be too hard to start it up again. I've saved up enough for me to find a nice quiet place in the Deadlands, far from anyone who might have a problem with someone in my line of work. Maybe take up some ridiculous hobby that old women do. Knitting.

Gambling. Maybe I'll buy a ship and fly to the edge of the galaxy. Hell, who am I kidding? I'll probably wind up as a Renegade info broker. We both know I can't help myself." She shrugged. "Or maybe I'll just take up fly fishing."

I narrowed my eyes. "You should get a cat. You don't know the first thing about fly fishing."

"I could *learn*," Pearl said, rather insistently. "How hard can it be?"

We both laughed.

"Well, I guess this is it, then," I said, after a bit of silence. "For both of us."

"I guess so, kid," she agreed, taking a sip of Mable's coffee. "You told the nun you were planning on leaving, is that right?"

I nodded.

"Getting away from everything is good," she told me.

"Helps you figure out your priorities. Wait, how much do you have saved up?"

I made a face. "Enough for at least a couple years of frugal spending. And when that runs out, I'm not exactly helpless. Worst case scenario, I can always become a nun like Mable did."

Pearl shook her head. "Are you kidding me?" she asked, almost disgusted. "Figures, you've always been soft like that."

"Look who's talking," I said, narrowing my eyes.

"I never asked to take care of a couple of kids," she said with a scoff.

"No, but you did a fine job, anyway." I smiled at her.

Pearl beamed, not hiding her satisfaction. She leaned over, placing a small pad on the table in front of me. On the screen, I spotted my picture on a passport file, along with a ticket for a shuttle that would be leaving the planet in a couple of hours.

I picked it up, examining my new identity.

My eyes fell on the name: Abigail Pryar.

I smiled.

"I'm still a little surprised you picked that name," Pearl said, leaning back into her seat. "What? Are you surprised Alec gave it up? You should have known I'd find out."

"The name felt right," I said, ignoring the question about Alec.

Pearl chuckled. "I don't think Mulberry ever had any kids. None that he ever told me about, which doesn't actually say much. But I think he'd be happy to know that you're the one that's going to be carrying his name forward. A part of his legacy. One of the best parts."

"Shut up," I grumbled, trying to roll my eyes as the smile remained on my face. "I don't want to start crying here."

"Then you might want to—" Pearl made a brushing motion on her cheek. I rushed my hand over my face. A tear had fallen without me even noticing. I cursed softly, pushing it away.

"It's fine, kid," Pearl said. "Sometimes it takes a long time to let it all out, and even then, maybe it doesn't really leave. That's the way it goes with loss, and now you know."

I placed the pad in my satchel and stood up. Pearl followed my lead, and we both went out into the street. As soon as the doors closed, I pulled her to me and hugged her close, the same way I had with Mable.

"Drop me a line when you're set up," I told her. "We can go fly fishing together."

"I'm rethinking that actually," Pearl said. "Sounds super boring. Probably just going to get a cabin in the woods. Hunt my dinner. Grow a beard. Start complaining about politicians. You know, that's the real life."

"Well," I said, pulling away with a laugh. "Whatever you end up doing, you just let me know. We can complain together."

Pearl grinned and leaned close to place a kiss on my cheek. "Will do, kid. In the meantime, you have yourself a good life. Make it better than the last one. Find your purpose, the way you always meant to."

"Thanks, Miss Pearl. You too," I said.

She smiled. "See you in the world, kid."

Epilogue

A soft feminine voice announced that boarding for the shuttle to Crescent had begun at gate eighteen. I picked my bag up from the floor and slung it over my shoulder. There weren't that many people headed to Crescent, so only a handful of others followed me as I approached the loading dock.

A pretty young woman with red hair greeted me with a smile and asked for my boarding pass. I handed it to her. She scanned it with a machine and handed it back with another smile.

"Enjoy your flight!" she said in an obviously forced, chirpy voice.

"Thanks," I replied with an equally forced smile as I stepped past her. I walked through the tunnel that led into the shuttle. It wasn't a big thing. Basically, a room with the passenger seats, complete with buckles and oxygen masks in case of emergency, and a lounge area with dispensers for drinks and food to be enjoyed on the way.

The cockpit and baggage areas were sealed off, only accessible by members of the crew which consisted of two pilots and three attendants. The three were directing passengers to take their seats and preparing for takeoff. Slipspace travel could be a bumpy ride.

I didn't really have much in the way of luggage other than some clothes, my pad, a few electronics, and the other bare essentials. Pearl had given me the contact information of a guy that could get me some weapons or armor on Crescent, should I need them, but I wasn't sure I would. Not for a time, anyway.

The artificial gravity locked in as the ship's engines started. The whole room shuddered as they started powering up, and after about a minute, we lifted off the ground. A brief second before the dampeners kicked in, I felt myself press back into my seat as we started gaining speed and altitude.

I looked out the window, watching Osiris fade with every passing second. This would be the last time I'd ever see this planet, and I had to say, I didn't' mind.

It only took us a few minutes to enter the stratosphere, and soon, we were in orbit. I leaned into my window, scanning the open space around us, watching the planet grow smaller in the distance. Even though I couldn't feel it anymore, I knew we were still accelerating.

The slip tunnel opening was halfway between this planet and the fifth, a barren world named Axti.

Fifteen minutes. That was how long it took before the pilot opened the rift. An anomaly in space that so few people understood and even the wisest of them only had fragments of knowledge. Slipspace, in all its emerald glory, lay before us.

I'd seen this sight before, but never had it looked so beautiful. Never had it been so freeing. It wasn't the way I'd wanted to do it, of course, but orphans couldn't be choosers.

The possibilities of my future were all before me. I could do anything. I could be anything.

I could be a nun, an assassin, a dancer, or an analyst. I could be a wife or a doctor, an actress or a vagabond. I could do them all or none, because finally, after all these years, I had a choice in how my life would unfold. I would be the master of myself, and I would never let anyone tell me otherwise.

As the tunnel tore open, and I saw the beautiful lightning crack across the inner green walls. I slipped my hand into my pack, pulling out my childhood pad, and I found a book.

Tales of the Earth: Mankind's Lost Homeworld.

I ran my fingers over the screen, staring at the title page.

I took a deep breath. I wasn't going to cry. Despite all the goodbyes, today was a joyful one. The first day of my life.

I smiled as the slip tunnel tugged at the shuttle, dragging us in. It started shaking the hull, and I could feel the now-familiar vibration as the tunnel started speeding us off toward Crescent. Green lights flashed across the windows. Emeralds made of light filled my view as I leaned back in my seat.

Once we were inside, the rest of the passengers unbuckled and started moving toward the lounge. I unbuckled too, but I stayed in my chair, tucking my knees up to my chest while putting the pad down on the table in front of me and flipping to the very first page.

It began with a small note:

Long ago, Mankind knew only one home. One world in all the universe to call its own. All races and creeds lived upon this rock, all vying for the same mound of dirt, knowing nothing of all the distant worlds still waiting to be found.

They called their lonely planet "Earth," and it was a place of true wonder. It was a realm of unimaginable history and human progress. Many say this is a myth. They claim it to be a legend, written by madmen and rehearsed by grandmothers in the late hours of the night.

But if you would listen, I would show you stories that would leave you in awe. Stories of plains as vast as oceans, cities that stretch across continents, and ships as big as moons. Stories of ancient history, of which we only have fragments, but which speak of great and wonderful things.

The Earth is out there, waiting for its children to return.

It waits for you and I both, dear Reader.

We need only reach out and believe.

-Dr. Darius Clare

AUTHOR NOTES

Nameless was a story I've wanted to write for some time, ever since Renegade Lost was released. Fans have been asking what Abigail Pryar's backstory was, and I wanted to tell them, but I wanted to do it justice with its own book. *Nameless* is the result of that.

Abigail's journey is one riddled with hardship and loss, but she chooses to move forward, no matter the situation. That is what makes her so compelling to me. It takes one hell of a woman to break into a government-controlled facility and rescue a little girl, as we see in *Renegade Star*, and now we know why.

I hope this story resonated with you, whether you're new to the Renegade universe or a seasoned reader. Either way, this story is meant to stand alone, adding to the overall mythology while also telling something entirely new.

I don't know if there will ever be more Abigail books, but there will undoubtedly be more Renegade stories with Abigail in them. If you're new to the series and would like to see more of this character, check out *Renegade Star* so that you can see the woman our little assassin becomes.

In the meantime, you can expect the 8th entry in the *Renegade Star* series, *Renegade Children*, to release this month (Oct. 2018), along with the premiere of a brand new series in the Renegade universe in early November, called *Orion Colony* (Nov. 4th, 2018).

As you can guess, I've got plenty of new tales to tell in this world, and they're all coming very soon.

Until next time, Renegades,

J.N. Chaney

Books By J.N. Chaney

The Variant Saga:

The Amber Project

Transient Echoes

Hope Everlasting

The Vernal Memory

Renegade Star Series:

Renegade Star

Renegade Atlas

Renegade Moon

Renegade Lost

Renegade Fleet

Renegade Earth

Renegade Dawn

Renegade Children

Nameless: A Renegade Star Story

Standalone Books:

Their Solitary Way

ABOUT THE AUTHOR

J. N. Chaney has a Master of Fine Arts in creative writing and fancies himself quite the Super Mario Bros. fan. When he isn't writing or gaming, you can find him online at www.jnchaney.com.

He migrates often but was last seen in Avon Park, Florida. Any sightings should be reported, as they are rare.

Nameless is his fourteenth novel.